A Blue Moon Interlude

BOOK I

Viji

First published in 2020 by

Becomeshakespeare.com

One Point Six Technologies Pvt. Ltd.
119-123, 1st floor, Building No. J2, Wadala East,
Wadala Truck Terminal, Mumbai, Maharashtra 400037, India
T: +91 8080226699

This book has been funded by WORDIT ART FUND
WORDIT ART FUND helps deserving
Authors publish their work
To apply for funding, please visit us at
becomeshakespeare.com

Editing by N. Jayalakshmi, Senior Associate Editor

Akshaya Venkataraman, Lawyer
Cover Design by Akshaya Venkataraman

©
ISBN 978-93-90040-87-2

DEDICATION

This work is dedicated to the state of Tamil Nadu and its ancient architecture

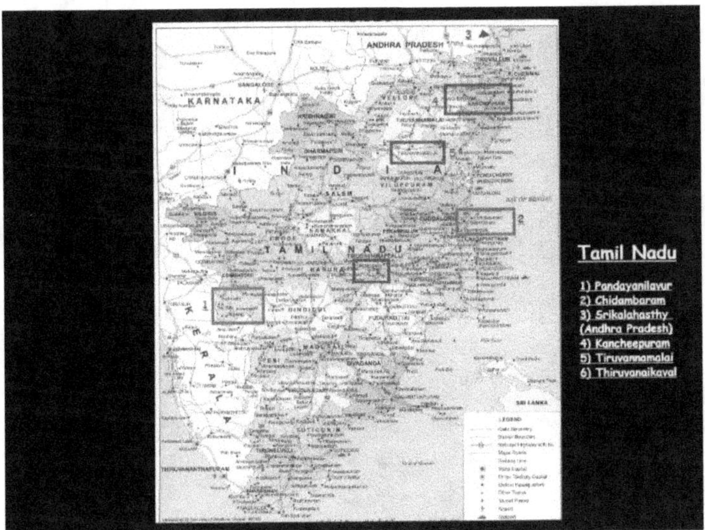

ACKNOWLEDGMENTS

To my mom & dad whose valuable advice and constant support motivates me to give my best.

To my husband who is my pillar of strength and whose confidence in me prodded me to continue with this endeavor.

To my sister whose invaluable guidance pushed me to continue my journey of 'A Blue Moon Interlude'.

To my mother-in-law whose words of encouragement boosted my morale.

To my brother-in-law whose assurance goaded me to begin this journey.

To my friends, cousins & family who supported me.

To Rajam Ananthakrishnan whose inputs on landscape architecture were very helpful.

And to my daughter Akshaya who is my inspiration, my critic and my teacher, and whose positivity gives rise to my creativity.

I would also like to thank and acknowledge the efforts of N.Jayalakshmi for editing and re-editing the work despite her busy schedule.

PREFACE

I have lived for many years in Chennai and while I was there, I was captivated by the Annual Car festival of Mylapore Temple. This festival is dedicated to 63 Nayanars, the Shaivite saints, who lived during the sixth-eighth centuries, and there was something timeless about the whole ritual that intrigued me. Thus, began my journey of researching into their life stories. Basing my plot on the life of one of the earliest Nayanars, I began writing this piece of fiction in May 2017 and completed in three years.

A Blue Moon Interlude

Oh! dear blue moon of the vast space,

Your interlude is awaited with grace,

By the lords and reformed, for you

Alone can bring sense to the few,

Who seek to discover the enigma.

Oh! dear blue moon of the wild yonder,

Your interlude is awaited with wonder

By your slaves and followers, for you

Alone can wither the attempts of the few

Who seek to perish the unknown key…

CONTENTS

PROLOGUE

THE VOW

"With wonder and astonishment, they watched in awe, the miraculous sight of him and his companion that unveiled before their eyes"- Thirumurai 12 (2-40)

6th Century (C.E)

Thillai Forest, Chidambaram

It was the month of *Margazhi* as per the Tamil Calendar and the gust of cold wind from the neighboring *Thillai* forest chilled their bones. Sixty-four years old Tiru Neelakanta shivered while he looked at his wife, Ratnasalai. Her face was pinched, and she stood stiff as the wind refused to abate. They were standing knee-deep in the *Pool* creating ripples around them.

Why was the Lord punishing them like this? Tiru Neelakanta looked at the spectators who had gathered around the water body. They were waiting eagerly for him to complete his penance. He hesitated to take his wife's hand in his. What about the promise he had made to her? Could he break the vow? The congregation of priests voiced their demand once again. They asked Neelakanta to follow the instructions of the ascetic standing at the head of the group. Neelakanta bowed to the ascetic and apologized, "Pardon me Lord, I cannot do as you say. Years ago, I took an oath and it would be a sin if I break it."

The ascetic asked, "What was the oath?"

"I promised my wife and my Lord *Neelakandar* that I would never touch her because I cheated on her once."

Everyone gasped in unison and glared at him with outrage. The priests huddled for a discussion and arrived at a unanimous decision. The head priest gave Neelakanta a stick and instructed, "Both of you hold two ends of the stick so that you will not touch each other and then prepare to go under the water."

A few days ago, the travelling ascetic had asked Neelakanta and his wife to safeguard his copper pot. Despite taking care of it diligently, the pot was not found when the *Yogi* came looking for it after his trip. Enraged with Neelakanta's carelessness, the holy man asked Neelakanta and his wife to drown in the *Pool* holding hands. Neelakanta had no qualms about serving the punishment; he would have gladly given up his life for the ascetic. But he wanted to mend his relationship with his wife before death separated them. Neelakanta looked at his wife with guilt and remorse. If only he had not succumbed to temptation all those years ago. That momentary weakness had wrecked his life and ensued immeasurable rift between him and his wife. He loved his wife and repented his sin.

He took the stick from the priest and asked his wife to hold one end, "I am really sorry Ratna. This would not have happened if I had been more careful in life. And you are the only one I love."

Teeth chattering in the sharp sting of the wind, Ratnasalai gave a wan smile. What did it matter? It was the end of their world. She wished she had not punished her husband so severely when he had cheated on her. She sighed and waited for her husband to dive into the water….

Together, they closed their eyes and chanted their Lord's name. They entered the water with closed eyes. When they rose up, they did not see the astonishment in the villagers' eyes.

A miracle was unfolding in front of the villagers. An unseen and unbelievable wonder! It was so unexpected and remarkable that the villagers were unable to comprehend it initially.

Tiru Neelakanta and his wife took another dip and when they were about to drown into the pool, the priests called out to them in incredulity…

"Neelakanta, open your eyes and look at you and your wife. This is a miracle…"

Tiru Neelakanta opened his eyes and looked at his wife. He stared in stunned appreciation.

It was not his sixty-year old wife who stood beside him but the beautiful young woman whom he had married years ago.

Ratnasalai looked as young as the day she had married him. Her youthful face and glowing skin caught his breath. His wife exclaimed, "Look at you! So young!"

It was then that Tiru Neelakanta looked at himself. His skin too glowed with vitality and freshness. It astonished him. How did this happen?

The villagers gathered around the pool and exclaimed,

"The water….The water in the Pool caused the miracle. Was it an elixir or medicine? Or was it the Lord's way of demonstrating his presence in the pool?"

The hushed murmurs of the villagers could be heard in the distant mangroves of *Pichavaram* and *Thillai forest*. Sometimes, miracles could never be explained by humans, but the swaying trees and rustling wind grasped the significant moment and unleashed their happiness by weaving through the village in their customary, joyous howls.

The wonderful event enhanced Tiru Neelakanta Nayanar's repute and the villagers established him as a devout man with allegiance to the Lord himself. They determined his status as the protector of the famed pool, and he vowed to conserve the *Pool* for eternity.

Since then, the Pool became famous as *"Ilamai Neerutru"* (Fountain of Youth)

THE VERSE

"Perceived only by the knowledgeable, unfathomed by logic, it is the genesis, the center and the ultimate"-Thirumurai 12 (1-1)

20th C.E (Year: 1994)

Kuala Lumpur, Malaysia

A few days earlier, some workers in Kuala Lumpur had stumbled upon the ruins of a Hindu temple when they were excavating for the construction of a new administrative capital called *Putrajaya*, south of Kuala Lumpur. At once, the administration invited historians and archaeologists to study and analyse the recovered materials.

The group of historians gathered at the sight to view the relics and study the idols, broken pillars and stone carvings. They scrutinized the sacred text and drawing to record the findings. There was a palpable air of excitement among the group. Arumugam Velu was one of the police officers in charge of security, and he was awestruck by the flag staff. It looked exactly like an enlarged version of the key he had received from his grand-uncle many years ago, prior to his uncle's death. The broken flag staff had a tiny bull in a sitting posture at the top. The pole was a unique piece among the ruins. He recalled his father telling him about *Kodi Marams* in his native land. He figured that the key was a miniature version of this *kodi maram.* His uncle had confided to him that the key was the '*sigichai sorgathin nuzhaivasal*' (the gateway to therapeutic haven) and now he marveled at the significant ancient key. He had heard fables about the key, but he had never thought he would get to see a larger version of the same. Was the mythical healing pool, mentioned in his uncle's letter under this debris? He took a closer look at the broken pole. The upper part of the flag-pole had designs engraved but the gold plating had peeled off at the edges and the bronze sheet was visible underneath. The lower part of the flag staff, which was thicker, had tiny multiple pillars built around the main pole. The middle part of the flag staff which lay separately, glittered in the sunlight. It was made of gold and this was the piece that interested Arumugam. He figured that the three pieces of the flag staff were made of different materials and that they had been assembled together for this temple. They were probably brought from different temples of South India. He peered at the central piece of the pole and tried to discern the words engraved in a corner. They were inscribed in the ancient language of Southern India and the words were in the form of a verse, arranged in a metrical rhythm. With a picture of it in his phone, he translated the verse at his house.

"The slave, who enchanted me, lives on this land, craved by the people, for worshipping…"

Arumugam compared the verse with the one his uncle had mentioned in his testimony. They were the same, both incomplete and unrhymed. He concluded that other parts of the same *kodi maram* would show the remaining verses. He was curious to discover if those other parts also lay under the same spot.

But, in the excavations during the following days, no one found any more remains of the flag staff. Nor did they find any remnants of a pool or tank. Arumugam was disappointed but reasoned with himself that it probably was only a mythical pool of water. Moreover, the state government of Tamil Nadu was demanding that Malaysia hand over the *Kodi maram* and idols to them. Arumugam was entrusted with the job of carrying the treasures to Chennai, given his proficiency in his native language Tamil, and his background as a police officer. Before departing for Chennai, he spoke for the last time to his sister residing in Fiji, not realising that he would never return to his adopted country.

He was heedless to the fact that someone was following him.

On his flight to Chennai, a man befriended Arumugam and the two of them – Arumugam and Raja Manickam, talked throughout the flight about their shared interest in Tamil history. When they landed in the city, they realised that Raja Manickam's luggage had not arrived with them and upon inquiries discovered that it would take another day to arrive. Taking pity on the fretting Raja Manickam, Arumugam offered his hotel room to Raja to stay in for the night, till his luggage arrived. When Arumugam awoke the next morning, a devastating shock awaited him. The state treasures and his documents had gone missing and Raja Manickam lay dead on the floor of the hotel room in a pool of blood. Arumugam, who was discovered at the scene of the crime, was arrested and charged with the non-bailable crime of murder. The investigation was rather swiftly concluded within three months and Arumugam was confined in a cell awaiting trial.

In the dark cell where he was confined, Arumugam was not aware of the days or years passing by. He missed his life in Kuala Lumpur and recollected the conversations between his sister and him. He yearned for the innocent chatter of his nephew Jeeva and for the companionship of his friends. He had no knowledge of the conspiracy that had framed him for the murder of Raja Manickam.

But he had faith in the judiciary, hoping that one day he would rightfully be given his trial.

THE VENDETTA

"During his reign, invaders from the north led a fierce battle with their enormous fleet of elephants against his cavalry" - Thirumurai 12 (50-3)

21st C.E (Year: 2004)

Chennai, Tamil Nadu

Udayarajan watched the interview on television. Arunachalam Chettiar, the powerful industrialist was being inundated with questions on his achievement. The Central Government had conferred the *'Corporate with Conscience'* award on one of the sister concerns of *'Thillai Group of Companies'*. Udayarajan had met Arunachalam once, but he had not been aware of his background. He had not known for instance that Arunachalam hailed from Chidambaram, though he should have guessed that from the name, *'Thillai'*. He listened with keen attention as the founder of the largest group of industries in Tamil Nadu- Arunachalam, spoke about his grand-father's initial days of struggle, "It was my grandfather who planted the seed of this empire. He had seen the worst that life could offer. Coming from a small village near **Aanaimalai hills*, he had to struggle to start life afresh in Chidambaram. Once his business started thriving, he shifted to Chennai."

Udayarajan was taken aback. He called up his brother Madhirajan in Indonesia. "Madhi, have you heard of Arunachalam Chettiar?"

"Who? Founder of 'Thillai Industries?"

"Yes, I was just watching his interview on television. Guess what he said."

"What?"

"That his grandfather hailed from a small village near *Aanaimalai hills…*"

"Really?"

"We should learn more about his background."

"Did he name our village?"

"No but I am going to dig into his ancestry."

****

Year: 2005

Chennai, Tamil Nadu

Nilagriva Chandra's classes concluded, and he strode quickly to the parking bay to start his two-wheeler. He did not notice the covetous glances that the girls gave his tall and handsome figure. The day was coming to an end and the traffic was growing at the peak hour. Nilagriva plugged in the earphones of his music player and rode the bike to his house. He did not hear his brand-new cell-phone, stuffed deep into his bag, ring.

Reaching home, he noticed the police vehicles and ambulance at the gate. He rushed inside and stopped dead. His family members were in a shock and some of them were wailing. The Para Medics were carrying down a body. He trembled in shock when he saw that it was his dearest cousin Shreekant. His mother was weeping, and his family was running helter-skelter. Nilagriva's brother who was three years younger had huddled around their mother looking scared. Nilagriva approached his mother,

"*Amma,* what happened?" His mother noticed him then and asked, "Nilu, how many times did I try calling you. Where were you? See what he has done…" She pointed out to the body and cried softly.

"But what happened? Tell me" He shook her.

"Shreekant committed suicide" She explained brokenly, and he froze in horror, a sudden chill sweeping through him.

He went closer to look at the body and he was appalled at the pale face of his cousin. He could not believe that his cousin had taken such a horrific decision. It was only in the morning that he had laughed with him and talked to him before leaving for school and Shreekant had been excited to go to college. He had even mentioned that he was planning to propose to the girl he was infatuated with. So why did he do this?

Nilagriva rushed to Shreekant's room on the first floor of the house, taking two steps at a time. He searched his cousin's room, but he could not find the gift Shreekant had purchased for the girl. So, had she accepted his proposal or not? While searching the room, he spotted a strange looking key lying below the cot. He picked it up but could not identify what the key was for or who the owner of the key was. He pocketed it, hoping to study it later, and kept looking for the gift that Shreekant had bought for his date. When Nilagriva could find nothing, he walked back to his room and opened the cupboard to deposit his bag. He was shocked.

The gift that his cousin had acquired for the girl was placed in his cupboard and there was a letter attached to it. Nilagriva opened the letter with trembling hands,

My dear Nilu,

You asked me to propose to her and I did but she refused. I would have continued with hopes but like always, you asked me to do something I didn't want to and look what happened....I hate you Nilu. I am leaving.

"Having enslaved myself to you, I realize you have shown my place..."

Shreekant

Nilagriva slumped on the bed with the sheet of paper quivering in his hands. The last line described his cousin's feeling for the girl very eloquently. He started crying. He felt vulnerable and broken. Someone knocked on the door and he looked up, rubbing away his tears quickly. It was his grandfather.

"Thatha...." He called out

His grandfather held him closely and confided, "I know. I kept Shreekant's note here."

Nilagriva looked at his grandfather in dismay,

"Yes, Nilu, he had placed the letter and gift on his own bed so that everyone would see it and blame you. Since I entered the room first and saw it, I hid it here..."

"Thatha, he died because of me." He wept in his grandfather's shoulder. At fifteen, he was as tall as his grandfather.

"No, it is not because of you. The girl must have misled him. Don't worry! No one knows about this note. Give it to me. I will destroy it."

His grandfather took the incriminating note, shred it into pieces and flushed it down the toilet. If he had not done it, the police would have taken Nilagriva for questioning.

They did not notice the man hiding behind the door in the balcony. He waited for them to leave so that he could search for his key locket. The police and servants were already swarming the premises however, so he abandoned his attempts to search for his key and escaped from the house.

THE VOW

PART - I

(21st CE – 2018)

1) CHIDAMBARAM

"Adorned with pearls, gems and gold, surrounded by men and women devotees with offerings of garlands, the glory of Arudra Darshan is unmatchable." Thirumurai 4(21-1)

Chidambaram

It was the ninth day of the *Thiruvadirai Festival* at Thillai Chidambaram and the *Maha Abhishekam* for Lord Nataraja and Goddess Sivakami would begin early the next morning. The crowd was swelling every hour and devotees travelled from different parts of the country to seek the blessings of the Lord during the *Arudhra Darisanam.*

Nedumaran Velan was huddled in a corner of the sprawling premises of the famed temple and counted the hours before the Full Moon would make its first glorious appearance for the year. And on this longest night of the year, Nedumaran would sing all the hymns praising the lord that his ancestors had taught him. Every year, he would sit alone in this corner beside the ancient water tank of the temple and chant those revered hymns. He would sing them while gazing at the full moon, imagining *Lord Nataraja* and *Goddess Sivakami* dancing in the cosmic luminance of the moonlight. And when the Lord and Goddess entered the *Kanaka Sabhai* after *Rahasiya Puja and Alangaram* to bless the devotees, Nedumaran would race to the old cottage near *Killai,* place his ear on the ground and listen to the flow of water beneath the ground. The trickle of water would make his heart swell with happiness and he would pluck flowers and fruits from the forest and adorn the spot on the ground. Then he would meditate for hours and try to recall the time-worn secrets that his ancestors had passed on to later generations.

But this year, he felt too weak and exhausted physically to race across the town. He had become frail over the years and his aged body refused to listen to his bodily commands. His predecessors had their descendants to continue the tradition of their sacred duties but Nedumaran had no progeny to pass on the deeply guarded secret. He devoted his solitary life to spiritual pursuits. And now, as he looked at the blue and azure sky, he realised that his end was approaching. An age-old instinct warned him of his last hours of journey on the earth. He closed his eyes and pondered. He had to divulge the undisclosed truth to the legatee. But how? There were already rapacious wolves on the hunt. If the knowledge of the mystic existence fell into the hands of the dubious, there would be catastrophe. He recalled his father's words that if any urgency or sudden necessity for the revelation arose, then he was to entrust the secret only to the heir apparent of the family that owned the dilapidated mansion and ancestral estate in *Killai.*

Nedumaran hurried back to his small and humble abode inside the layout of the estate. The large area was chiefly covered with trees and undergrowth. He opened the door of his thatched room and made his way to the loose slab next to his bed, under which lay an old copper box. He lifted the slab slowly and removed the box. Dusting it with a towel, he unlocked the lid and peered inside. His fatigued eyes could not find it immediately, but he lit the inside of the box with a torch and found the odd-shaped key. There was a leaf with a couplet written on it. He wrapped the key in the leaf and sealed it inside an envelope. He took another piece of shriveled sheet, frayed at the ends from the box. He scrutinised the address written on the sheet closely and copied it on the envelope. He wrapped the envelope in a piece of cloth and put it in another thick, brown and larger cover. To his untraveled mind, wandering out of Chidambaram with the classified knowledge was like being stranded in the midst of a churning ocean. He decided to send the envelope by post. He rushed out in hurry for only one hour remained for the post office to close for the day. At the post office, he weighed the envelope, paid the amount and sent it through speed post. Finally, he had unburdened himself of the obligation that he had cradled deep in his heart.

The vast space above Thillai Chidambaram was slowly and steadily preparing itself for the glorious night. Like the royal cavalcade that would precede the real appearance of the majesty, the stars twinkled and glittered before the moon arose in its dazzling silhouette.

He strolled back to the temple and awaited the grand celebrations of the tenth day of the festival. He stroked his long white beard and settled down at his usual spot. He started crooning the hymns and a small crowd gathered around him to listen to his renditions.

He looked up at the lush, violet sky and gazed at the Full Moon that appeared in all its splendour. He closed his eyes and prayed,

"Dear Blue Moon, please deliver my message to its authentic keeper. Do not allow it to get into the hands of the depraved. The wolves are already hunting for it and murdered a young man for it. The promise I made to my father must not dissipate."

His mind summoned up the image of the boy who used to come to Chidambaram often in search of the dreaded substance. The youth was addicted to it. Nedumaran had advised him many times to tread carefully. But his counselling had fallen on deaf ears. Then he had learnt that the boy had committed suicide. He was certain that there was something more sinister behind the death than was obvious.

In the packet that he had sent to the family today, he had penned a small note, confiding the truth about their boy. It happened many years ago and Nedumaran had waited for the heir of the family to appear at Chidambaram so he could entrust the sacred testimony to him. But now that Nedumaran was on the cusp of life and death, he did not want to risk the inevitable.

****

Chennai

The city of Chennai in the Coromandel coast of the Bay of Bengal sparkled with lights as the sun started to set in the far west. Sindhoora was so engrossed in her assignment that she didn't observe the sunset or the daylight transforming to twilight. The incense sticks fragrance drifted to her and she realised that the day had come to an end. The classes had wrapped up some time ago and she left the tiny room on the first floor of the commercial building to climb down the dark and narrow steps exiting towards the bustling and crowded street of the area. Her friend Vidya joined her as she finished her music classes on the ground floor. Together, they walked down the streets towards their houses. The evening *deepa aradhana* at the historical Shiva temple of *Mylapore* was taking place and they could hear the loud gong of the temple bells. The sound reverberated across the hub of the metropolis and Sindhoora felt serene and peaceful. Her mood always lifted a notch higher after hearing their chimes. Somehow, she felt a timeless wonder at these peals of the bells.

The shops were lit brightly, and people bumped against one another to buy vegetables from the hawkers. It was difficult to walk on the footpath with so many carts and vendors occupying it, but Sindhoora did not mind the inconvenience. She loved the hustle and bustle of the area. The shops and market around the temple tank were always thronged by one and all. They housed every little thing needed for daily use.

Rows of houses flanked the huge fort like walls of the temple on all its four sides, branching into narrow streets called *Agraharams*. Sindhoora's house was situated in one such street.

Sindhoora's mobile phone vibrated. There was a new message from *#ChennaiWhiteKnights*, a group that she was a member of.

"Guys we need to meet immediately. It is urgent. Assemble at our usual point." Sindhoora frowned at the message and checked the time. It was almost six thirty. Her mother would be waiting for her, but it was also necessary to attend the meeting. She sighed, "Vidya, I have to go for a meeting. I will take a bus from this stop."

"But Sindhu… at such short notice?"

"I know but I have to be present. See you tomorrow." Sindhoora bid her friend goodbye and hurried to the bus stop. While she waited for the city bus, she called up her mother to tell her about the meeting,

"Sindhu, how will you come back? It will get late."

"Don't worry *amma*. I will ask one of my friends to drop me."

****

Akhil waited impatiently for Sindhoora. Most of the other members had already arrived and he was definite that Sindhoora too would show up for the meeting. They had gathered at a park which also served as a milk booth and café. It was at the center of *Adyar* junction. The discussion had already begun and Akhil's searching eyes wished for Sindhoora's presence. With a relieved sigh, he spotted her stepping out of the bus and walking towards the park.

Her *Paavadai* and short cotton Kurti was traditional but they were trendy. Maybe Sindhoora's attire was standard but she looked quite stylish in the dress with a short single plait that she placed casually in the front over her right shoulder. Her jute bag and jute sandals enhanced her look.

Akhil noted that her slender figure with confident stride attracted some attention on the road. Some of the young boys gave her second looks while older men stared at her unabashedly as she jostled her way through the crowd and traffic to the park.

"Sindhu…."

Sindhoora sighted her cousin Akhil and bonded happily with her friends. These young adults of the same age-group had formed this body called *#ChennaiWhiteKings* when they had been at school. Originally, a small group of three boys and two girls, the body had now grown into a club of thirty members. They crusaded against anything that they deemed harmful to the environment. A couple of years ago, they had protested against the construction of monuments at the famous Marina beach. Today, they assembled for a different cause.

"Hi Sindhu…" Sindhoora had known most of them since school.

"What is so urgent Giri?"

"Ok! Let me start. You guys must have heard of or seen this ancient water tank near *Thiruvanmiyur*? The tank was temple property earlier but now I am not certain. My source has confirmed that there is a plan to seal the tank and use the space for public car parking. "

"What?" The members chorused their disapproval against the plan…

"That is so dumb."

"Yes, especially when there is perennial water crisis in the city!"

"Exactly! The admin is so dense."

"I agree. Imagine what it will do to the resource…"

"Their explanation is that the tank has been dry for many years and that slum dwellers use it for their personal purpose which renders it unhealthy."

"So, if that is the case then they can carry out rain harvesting or find a way to channel water from other sources to the tank."

"They have to clean it first and then begin the restoration."

Giri intervened, "Guys guys stop… First of all, we have to protest against the plan for a car parking area over it. We can't allow them to destroy the tank like this. You guys gather as much people as you can and make placards. I have a friend in the press. He will cover it. If any one of you have connections in the electronic media, invite them over to shoot the demonstration live."

"When are we assembling for the protest?"

"Sunday will be the best time. We will be free from work and we can direct the attention of the public to the cause."

"We should have an alternative plan for the dried tank. We can't just protest and walk away. We will have to give reasons for our demonstration and show some ideas for restoration," Sindhoora suggested.

"Yes Sindhu. Sharan can point out the reasons for our protest and Sindhu; you can comment on the restoration. After all, you are the one working for landscaping architects." Giri reminded her of the company she was working for. Sindhoora agreed to the plan.

With the discussion coming to an end, they hung around the park for some time relishing the ice creams and milk shakes. Sindhoora was too busy exchanging notes with others to notice Akhil admiring her. She was unaware that, for Akhil, her wish was his command. He has been in love with Sindhoora for ages and he didn't remember a time when he had not been in love with her. But he had not yet plucked up the courage to confess to her. Every night, he would watch old films of his favourite hero of Tamil Cinema, *Kamal Haasan,* to come up with novel ideas. He had no clue whether she too nurtured similar feelings for him. Many times, he had tried to question her brother about it but Adithya always disregarded his queries. Akhil decided to express his feelings to her soon.

Akhil observed her heart-shaped face that belied her strong-willed nature although her determined jaw gave her away. Often, when she was in deep thought, her soft dark eyes took on a sharp glint that made people take her more seriously, than the feminine picture that she impressed upon them unknowingly, allowed them to. Despite her intelligence, she was naive in matters of the heart and this quality of Sindhoora made an impact on some men. A potent combination that she was unaware of, but it caused her mother sleepless nights.

Now, Akhil offered to drop Sindhoora home and as she rode with him on his bike, she marveled at the expanse of the night sky. She spotted an aircraft leaving a white trail behind. Other than Sudoku and chess, another of her favourite hobby was aircraft spotting! Every night after dinner, she would go to the terrace and spot planes. Then, surfing on the internet she would trace the plane to its destination. She would note down the flight path and name of the airline. Somehow flights and their journeys fascinated her and each time she would promise herself to travel by the same flight in future. Her brother teased her that her obsession for travel stemmed from the fact that she had not stepped out of Chennai in all her twenty-three years. Except for one summer vacation at Coimbatore when they had been very young, Sindhoora spent all her growing up years in Chennai.

As the brightest star twinkled on the dark midnight blue sky, she promised herself that there would come a time when she would also board those planes.

2) THE DIVINE SLAVES

"Enslaved to you forever, I cannot disclaim or disguise my devotion to you ever." Thirumurai 7 (1-1)

When the message alert on his phone sounded, Udayarajan checked the message…

"24.8318° N, 79.9199° E."

****

He instructed his assistant, "Book my ticket on the next flight."

Udayarajan travelled to a small town called *Khajuraho* in the *Bundelkhand* region of the state of Madhya Pradesh while his brother, Madhirajan who had flown to New Delhi from Indonesia was driving down from the capital. Udayarajan reached *Khajuraho* when the first rays of the sun touched the rising spire of the east-facing temples. As he awaited his brother's arrival, he looked out of the French window of his hotel room. The barren and stark land, basking in the morning warmth, had inspired great builders to erect towering monuments. Udayarajan pondered over the reason for the *Chandela Dynasty* rulers to choose this site for the magnificent and iconic temples. The temples were preserved from the medieval period of India and the famed temple of Lord *Mahadeva* where the congregation would be held was only one of the many monuments of the town. He presumed that during the 9th and 10th century, the area around the Vindhya ranges might have been richer and more lush influencing the rulers to choose the town for the architectural grandeur.

Udayarajan and his brother were present in the town to attend the gathering of *"Celestial Verses"*. A new member was to be admitted into the group and he had already proved his allegiance to the sect by overthrowing the ruling political party of an island nation. As a principle, the group never revealed the location of their meeting. They messaged the co-ordinates of the place to all its members and it was up to the members to track the place.

The new member was a retired chief of the naval force of the island nation and he had helped the rebels stage a coup to bring down the government. The rebels had conferred the power of their country to a man who was known to be secular and progressive. Very few realized that behind the closed doors of his room, the leader was a religious zealot who could force feed an entire generation to believe that the supreme power rested in *Mount Kailash* and in the Lord whose abode it was.

Each member of the group called *'Celestial Verses'* defined himself as the divine slave of the Lord. If a new member was to join the group, then he would be given a couple of months to prove his worth before he accepted the role of the divine slave. There were forty-nine of them and with the addition of the newest member, it would be fifty. Everyone's informal title was used by the sect for communication.

Udayarajan admired the countless figures of idols sculpted and fitted into the many niches in the outer structure of the *Mahadeva* temple. *'Celestial Verses'* always chose a temple of Lord Shiva to conduct their clandestine meetings and this time the *Mahadeva* temple of *Khajuraho* was chosen as their venue. The porches and towers which rose to a spire were very dissimilar from the temples in South India, while the spires were a common feature in the temples of Central India especially ones that were built after the tenth century. The imperial architecture reminded him of the glorious past of the town followed by the decline and decay afterwards. The group assembled at one of the many chambers inside the temple.

Udayarajan acknowledged each one in the group. If one member was the head priest of a temple in the island nation of the Indian Ocean who was called *'The Pearl'* by the sect, then another was a spiritual leader known as *'The Shark'* who amassed wealth like it was no one's business. He belonged to one of the East Asian countries. Then there was the media mogul who could topple any political party and whose empire spawned a large chain of print media publications, a thriving TV network and one of the world's largest digital media platforms. He was *'The Deep Sea'*. There was a cricketing legend, *'The Octopus'* who was an established maniac and whose on-field accomplishments matched those of his off-field stunts. His weakness was nubile young girls. *'The Blue Whale'* was the head of a political party vying for power and he was known as a dictator. *'The Pirate'* was an industrialist from the south whose reach spanned all the continents. Udayarajan, who was also a member of the *'Celestial Verses,'* was called *'The Coral'*. They were all very powerful and influential men who had the best of collective resources at their disposal. Their common goal was to identity self with the Supreme Lord *Shiva* and the belief that they were free from transmigration.

The world was unaware that they were also fanatics who were uncompromising in the pursuit of their ideals. Their mission was a unified world that believed in their Lord as the Supreme Power of the Universe. Lord *Shiva*, Lord *Mahadeva*, Lord *Neelakanda*, Lord *Nataraja,* one power with many names. He was their Lord Supreme and their conviction that they would establish a new world order inspired consecutive generations of the divine slaves. Many conspiracy theories followed the group in the past. It was alleged that they manipulated the economy of the country, eliminated radicals who opposed religious superstitions, and had involved in cloud seeding technologies that triggered floods in certain regions. Some believed that artificially created viruses were planted to eliminate communities who did not believe in the Supreme Lord. Theorists also claimed that the Tsunami that killed many and wiped out an entire island a decade ago had been triggered by a detonated bomb that had been implanted at the behest of *'Celestial Verses'* at an underground tunnel, constructed in another nation. Confounding theories of conspiracy raged around the secret sect, but no one had knowledge of the members or had found any evidence to prove their theory. The sect that had been existent for many centuries followed the rules laid down by their predecessors.

Udayarajan was the founder of a company called *'The Bay's Architects'* in Chennai. It specialised in landscape architecture. There was another motive for Udayarajan's founding the company. Under the guise of landscaping, he would unearth prized and inestimable treasures and antiques during the course of his projects. His brother Madhirajan owned a pharmaceutical lab in Indonesia. Together they formed a group of bounty hunters who smuggled antiques from India and sold them at the global black market. Their network was wide and untraceable.

Madhirajan joined his brother to watch the initiation of the newest member. As the most powerful men gathered inside the dark chamber of the medieval temple, they pledged to spread the message of the *Nayanars*. They passed around a tiny sealed container made of copper, inside which, was the chemical element called Mercury, commonly known as quick silver. Back in the ancient times, the enlightened men considered Mercury as a sacred and undisputed core of all metals, also believed to be the semen of Lord *Shiva*. The earliest scriptures elucidated in detail the benefits of the powerful substance. Hence, all the meetings of *'Celestial Verses'* never concluded without paying obeisance to it.

The retired general promised to adhere to the secrecy of the sect, and he was pronounced as '*The Viking*' by the head of the gathering.

The monarch of a mountain kingdom who called himself, '*The king maker*' started speaking, "We have been searching for that elusive knowledge that has evaded us for hundreds of years. We all know that multiple researches on ancient Indian medicine resulted upon a secret verse from an ancient text of the *Rasaveras* that points out, when the universe is spiraling towards a catastrophe, only a pool of spring water that shields a golden *lingam* can save the world with its elixir. Thanks to our doctor here who discovered the old scripture after years of research."

Udayarajan glanced at the doctor, *The Lagoon*. He was a well-known neurosurgeon in an elite hospital in the United Kingdom. The medical forums invited him often for their conferences across the world. The doctor explained, "The gold of the *lingam* acts as the alchemy in the water and when the water of the pool mixes with mercury, its potency will cure most of the diseases. We can take our planet back to the golden age."

"Where is this pool of water?" *The Pirate* asked. Udayarajan observed the industrialist who hailed from the south. He was soft-spoken and mild-mannered, and everyone liked him. But Udayarajan knew that beneath that gentle exterior; was a ruthless and power-hungry person who would go to any length to meet his goal. Udayarajan admitted the fact that each one in the group, including him, strove for absolute power in the name of the Lord.

"We have to search for the pool of water. We don't need a seer or spiritual guru to do miracles. When we discover the pool, it would be the Supreme Lord who would be performing the miracles. Imagine what it would do to our faith? We will be the undisputed

Caliphs lording over the universe."

"*Om namah shivaya*" he chanted, and the others followed. The dark chamber with carved stone pillars and steadfast walls echoed the sound.

"The text also mentions that the body of water exists deep under a forest in the land between two seas. We can think only of south India which is the land mass between two seas."

"It could be an island too," the cricket legend suggested.

"But islands are surrounded by sea. It is not between two oceans or seas."

"So how do we go about it? We can't go digging for it," Udayarajan asked

"Forest fires…….." *The Kingmaker* made the suggestion in a conspiratorial whisper.

"Forest Fires?"

"Yes. We start forest fire over a particularly dense range of forest. When the fire subsides, we could take up the contract to clear the debris and thus explore our way through them."

"There are too many forests in the south."

"Exactly and my gut instinct tells me that it lay underneath one of them. Udayarajan, you know the area well. Why don't you suggest?"

"We could start the process during peak summer. The dry spell and windy conditions could make it vulnerable. Such factors would make it look natural. But the problem is there would be a lot of trekkers, vacationers during that period."

"Let there be casualties. Only then will they give permission to the region. The media should be able to access it so that they can carry the stories in the headlines. What do you say Jagan?"

"Bringing it to public attention would be suicidal for us." Just like Udayarajan, Jagan, known as '*the deep-sea*', was also a native of Tamil Nadu.

"No, when there is too much attention, the administration would be in a hurry to make progress and the contract would be tendered without much delay."

"There is another way too to go about this," Udayarajan suggested. "We can build resorts and landscape some of the areas which will allow us to search for buried water bodies."

"You are forgetting the so-called environmentalists. They oppose constructions everywhere. They would not allow us to touch the forests."

"We need to carry out a campaign to show the particular piece of land as barren and infertile. Leave it to me but it will take time," Udayarajan made the proposition.

"Yes, it might take us a couple of years, but we have to start somewhere. And yes, there was one more interesting thing that the doctor discovered in the texts of the *Siddhars.*"

The members of the group looked at the doctor curiously while he regarded each one of them thoughtfully.

"It was believed that the *Pool of healing water* was shielded by one of the earliest *Nayanars* and his descendants guarded over it later. During the invasion of rulers from the north, they sealed the pool with many structures over it. There were keys to every slab of the construction above the pool and without the keys it is not possible to access the pool."

"So, who has the keys?"

"Well, that is the problem here. We don't know if the keys exist now. But if they do, then who owns them? The keys might have disappeared over the passage of time. Or there might be a group of people who are still protecting it. We will have to search for them."

The kingmaker added, "The uniquely shaped keys had five replicas."

The members were unaware that one among them possessed one of the five keys that they called the '*Sigichai sorgathin nuzhaivasal*' (Gateway to therapeutic haven). But he did not reveal his secret. It was his weapon to wield when the need arose. He was already searching for the *Pool of healing water*. He had the resources and he believed that he was the one destined to discover it.

The discussion went on for hours and when the sun started to dip in the west and the shadows lengthened on the walls made of sandstone, the group dispersed after fixing a month for the next meeting.

Local legends from time immemorial held the view that this temple town nestled in the lap of the Vindhya ranges and set amidst local hills and rivers, was the favourite place for Gods to play. The Gods enjoyed visiting the dramatic hill formation and umpteen water bodies that included lakes and ponds, many of which were not visible now.

The fascinating history of *Khajuraho* depicted through the carvings and murals bespeak of many dynasties that have risen to power in the medieval town. The kings and rulers during their reign built astonishing monuments, reflected their love and passion for the forbidden art through erotic sculptures, and recorded their legacy through the manifestation of spectacular temples for some of the most revered gods of Hinduism and Jainism. Historical records show invasions, destructions, desecration and neglect of the group of monuments. Over the centuries, vegetation and forests overgrew, taking over the temples, concealing them for many centuries before they were rediscovered. Through the span of various epochs, these monuments have stood tall, enduring the cruelty and greed of man and his lust for power. Some of the temples were restored and some of them lay in ruins even now. There has been a widely accepted belief that a number of *Yogis* and *Siddhars* still live in some of these temples of the lost world.

The monuments shrunk into the dark shadows of the dusk gradually as the sun set for the day. The staggering pillars had witnessed the pinnacle of glory, exemplary grandeur and bloody wars from one era to another. The land that they stood on had been worshipped, abused and mutilated by the savagery of men. But never have they seen a generation willing to commit atrocities in the name of the Lord or conduct genocide to wipe out a set of population. Man had become a pawn in the hands of the bloodthirsty as the battle lines between the good and the bad narrowed dangerously. Redemption had no place in the world. In the garb of god and religion, faith and trust were shred into twisted whorls of evils.

3) NILAGRIVA CHANDRASHEKHAR

"Praising you, the favourite of the wise bull and whose tusk reflects the sageness and knowledge."　　　*Thirumurai 10-1*

Zurich, Switzerland

Neel was crossing the transit gate of the airport when he realised that his laptop bag weighed much lighter than before. He checked his bag and realised that his bag had been switched. He lifted the flap of the bag and to his consternation found his laptop missing.

He swore and notified one of the officials about his missing laptop. He informed them that it was in his possession when he was alighting from the international flight that he had boarded at John F Kennedy Airport.

"Neel what is it?" his girlfriend Ann who was accompanying him from New York to India asked him.

"Someone has stolen my laptop."

"But you were working on it in the flight."

"Yeah, I know. That is what I am explaining to these guys." His other friends Mike and Rahul were following them and waiting a few feet away in the queue.

Neel's long overcoat was given back to him and he checked for his passport and other documents. The officers took them to the cabin for the *'Lost and Found'*. While the officers made enquiries about his laptop, Neel looked outside the window at the dull and grey late evening. Winter had arrived earlier in this part of the world. The evening mist made it difficult for him to admire the snow-capped ranges of the Alps, which he knew would be visible on a clear day.

He had visited Zurich many times. In fact, he doubted whether there was any place in Europe which he had not visited. And he always chose Zurich as the transit hub while travelling to India because it was more efficient in comparison to other airports. Today, the long flight from New York to Zurich was not very smooth. They chanced upon more turbulence than usual and by the time they crossed the Atlantic, his body had felt like it had been through a roller coaster ride. He knew it was an exaggeration because he was pre-occupied by his forthcoming visit to his family and home. It normally made him tense and irritable.

Ann barged into the office followed by Mike and Rahul. "Hey, how did you lose it? We were standing right behind you. How could they have switched the bag like this?" Mike asked him

Neel shrugged his shoulder and replied, "I don't know. I have heard that it is common to lose your laptops in this region. Thankfully all my important documents and cards are with me in this coat." He patted the pocket of his oversized jacket.

"Is it possible to recover it?" Rahul asked as Ann tried to speak to the officials in her broken German. She turned back to Neel and said, "Neel, they don't have much hopes of getting it back. We will have to fill this form for their verification."

Neel filled the form with personal information; he paused at the name box. He wrote the name stated in his passport, '*Nilagriva Chandra Shekhar*'.

Three hours later, Neel and his friends were back on another flight that was bound for Chennai. They could not track down his laptop although the officials said that they would message him if they located it. But no one had much hope of finding it. Gadget thefts especially of laptops were rampant in this part of Europe. People often lost them in trains, buses and public places. There was a huge market for stolen gadgets and thieves were very quick. They would change hands deftly without any delay. The officer who was helping Neel at the Airport in Zurich informed him that laptops go missing every fifty seconds or so.

As the flight took off from Zurich, Neel leaned across the window to get a glimpse of the Alps. Tiny lights glittered from the small hamlets in the valley and he could see vast stretches of snow-capped slopes. Soon the place would be filled with tourists keen on winter sports.

Neel knew that it would be very difficult to crack the password of his laptop and only an experienced hacker could do it. He turned around to look at Ann as she snuggled deeper into his shoulder, catching his attention. He noticed that his other two friends, sitting in the row across the aisle were fast asleep.

"What are you thinking Neel?" Ann asked him softly, caressing his unshaven stubble. She took pleasure in stroking his soft and crisp long hair at his nape. Ann and Neel had known each other for five years but he was still an enigma to Ann. She could never fathom his thoughts behind those dark hooded eyes. With high cheek bones, thick and straight black hair and brooding eyes that penetrated one with their intense stare, Neel Chandra was one of the most handsome men she had met. Tall and lithe, with a seemingly indolent attitude and an aloof stance, he drew girls to him quite easily with his allure. Ann became friends with him when they were at University and later she became his partner in the firm that he founded three years ago. His tall figure and tanned skin had made him stand out in their campus. He drew attention wherever he went with an easy charm that required no effort on his part. Ann would tease him about it, and he would look amused and shrug it off.

Sometimes, she speculated if there was anything that would rock the perpetual control he had over his emotions.

Now as she waited for his answer, she grazed her lips across his bristled jaw line. There was no change in his attitude, and he gave her a dry glance reading her mood accurately.

"I was thinking about my family's reaction to your arrival," he said with a sheepish smile and added, "I have not informed them about you accompanying me."

****

In the small chalet outside Zurich, the men cursed and tried to crack his password. They had to find the password quickly before the cops traced the laptop. But it seemed impossible. Unlike other stolen gadgets that were resold immediately into the black-market, this laptop was robbed for an entirely different purpose. The two men had been stalking Nilagriva for the last three weeks in New York. They had followed him till Zurich. But now they were at a dead-end.

****

"What? That is so mean of you Neel," Ann said, punching him on his shoulder and added anxiously, "Why didn't you tell your family? Are you afraid of their reactions?"

Neel turned his face to take in her expression and noticed her anxiety. Strands of ash blond hair were sticking out of her woolen cap and her grey eyes narrowed in tension. He drew in his breath and explained, "Ann, I don't know why I didn't tell them. It has nothing to do with you. I thought I would explain in person about your tour and work."

Accepting his explanation, she laid her head on his shoulder and tried to sleep. The lights dimmed and he turned to look out of the window. The ocean below glistened under the starry night and his thoughts strayed back to the awful year when his cousin Shreekant had committed suicide. It still brought shudders to him.

After his grandfather found out about the suicide note, he had made sure to keep the cops from approaching or suspecting Neel. The matter had been suppressed and the family had concluded that since Shreekant took drugs, it had caused momentary aberration and he had taken the extreme step.

Only his grandfather and Neel knew the truth behind the suicide. The incident had depressed Neel with life. He had tried to find the girl who had rejected his cousin, but she had left town. Neel's grandfather decided to send him abroad for higher studies so that he would try to forget the traumatic episode.

But Neel grew up never forgetting the bitter words of his cousin. It made him question the meaning of relationships and family. He changed his name from Nilagriva to Neel Chandra. He hated it if someone called him Nilu because it would bring back the memories of the last note his cousin had left for him. Slowly his family also started addressing him as Neel or Neel Chandra. Though he was Nilagriva Chandra Shekhar officially, he was better known as Neel Chandra. He had spent the last thirteen years in Europe and USA completing his studies and getting work experience. Three years ago, he founded his own company with the help of two of his college friends. Ann joined him one year later. It was now one of the leading firms that developed software for various companies for their entire employment cycle, including payroll, employee recruitment, retirement, etc. The firm was growing rapidly and in three years, there were more than fifty people employed in it.

He was aware that his grandfather, father and uncles anticipated his return eagerly and wanted him to join their multi-core family business. He was the heir apparent to *'Thillai Group of Industries'* and he hailed from an illustrious, rich and powerful Chettiar family in Chennai. But he had no wish to return to his native city. He planned to tell his family about his decision during this trip. He knew he was the apple of his grandfather's eyes, but he could not think of returning to a normal life in that house. The bitter memories refused to be erased from his mind. And every time he looked at his aunt, Shreekant's mother, he felt remorse eating him up. He had made a life of his own in another country and he hoped to convince his family about it.

Mike and Rahul were his college friends and they had wanted to tour India, so they decided to travel with Neel. He had made many friends in the intervening years abroad and he had been in many relationships, but nothing lasted much. He did not commit himself to any relationship deeply and never let anyone affect him emotionally. He called on his family in Chennai only when his mother or grandfather insisted on it. With thoughts from the past overcrowding his mind, Neel drifted into a fitful nap as the flight soared ahead into a different time zone.

****

Chennai

The sprawling bungalow called *'Chidambaram Illam'* at one of the posh localities of Chennai, namely *Alwarpet,* wore a festive look and there were workers moving about the house with garlands, flowers and lights. The women of the house draped in *Kanchivaram* silk sarees were overseeing the sweets, *prasadams* that were being made in the large kitchen. The family Guru or *Acharya,* as he is fondly called, was arriving from Chidambaram that day and the patriarch of the family, Arunachalam, was busy with preparations for the Guru's arrival and the *Puja* thereafter. Later on, his grandson Nilagriva was arriving from USA. So, it was a double celebration at the Chidambaram house. Arunachalam's imposing personality was not visible in any of his sons. In a white crisp *Veshti* and *Khadi silk kurta*; he looked a picture of authority in the Chidambaram household. Coming down the steps, he observed his children in different sections of the living area. His elder son Chandra Shekhar and second son-in-law were discussing matters of the company. His eldest daughter Saraswathy, who had lost her son to drug addiction a few years ago, was busy instructing the chefs about pure ghee sweets for the *Puja*. His two daughters-in-law and the youngest daughter were assisting the Priest. His second son had gone to fetch the *Acharya* from Chidambaram.

He frowned; none of his grandchildren were seen. Sometimes they were too modern for his lifestyle and at other times they followed him obediently. As he climbed down, he looked at the portrait of his wife who died five years ago, leaving him with the mammoth task of guiding their children. How he wished she was alive to share this moment of Nilagriva's arrival! He was proud of all his grandchildren, but Nilagriva held a special place in his heart. Arunachalam sighed wistfully. If his other grandson Shreekant had not blamed Nilagriva for his suicide then Nilagriva would have grown up in this house. But the traumatic incident had driven his favourite grandson into depression and Arunachalam had sent him abroad to avoid the harrowing aftermath. He was aware that the distressing episode had affected Nilagriva greatly.

Nilagriva's mother Revathi and father Chandra Shekhar had been unhappy about Arunachalam's decision to send their son away for higher studies, but no one argued with Arunachalam. His decisions were unanimously accepted in the *Chidambaram Illam*. As the founder of the *'Thillai Group of Industries'* he wielded enormous power and influence. Now his sons and son-in-law were taking care of the flagship. He hoped that as scion of the group of industries, his grandson Nilagriva would start being at the helm of the company affairs.

****

Killai, Chidambaram

Faraway from Chennai, the stillness of the midnight was broken by the droning of motorboats. When they neared the coastline, the motors were switched off and they towed the boats to the shore. The silvery halo of the moonlight guided the men to clear the boats of the stacked crates and stow them on the marshy wetlands between the shrubs. There were five boats with ten crates each and by morning the crates would have disappeared from the groves into the towns. If one opened the crate, one could find tender coconuts of export quality packed inside. They were transported from Myanmar, packed in Laos and shipped from Thailand. Away from the territorial waters of the state, where the contiguous zone made it difficult to impose the law of the nation, deals were cracked, and the consignments were shipped. Inside the tender coconuts were packed white powder which carried the consumers to new heights of euphoria. By the time the earliest rays of the sun grazed the thick groves, the consignment would have left the wetlands and transported to different corners of the country.

The leader of the team checked if all the crates had been unloaded from the boats. The marshy soil was drawing them in, but their boots helped them to hold on to the twisting roots of the mangroves. Once their task was complete, they would sail back to the abandoned island near Port Blaire. They would spend the night among the ruins of the island and head back east by mid-morning.

They did not have to worry about food in the isolated island. There were plenty of deer and variety of birds for them to grill on the open fire. The dilapidated old church made a perfect setting for their night-cap.

4) THE HOMECOMING

"To all those who love you; you are omnipotent." Thirumurai 8 (1-1)

Nedumaran watched the furtive activity from the other corner of the beach. Sleep eluded him and the frequent load shedding of power made it impossible for him to sleep. Hence, he had taken a stroll to the beach. Sitting under a palm tree, his aged eyes noticed the boats arriving. These nocturnal ventures had been happening for many years now, but no one dared to stop them. Even if the law enforcing officers were aware of it, they had turned a blind eye. Five years ago, an honest officer who had been transferred to the town stumbled upon these unauthorised movements in the mangroves and had complained about it to higher authorities. But a month after he lodged the complaint, he had gone missing. No one learnt whether the office shifted him, or he left the town of his own volition. He had disappeared one fine morning.

As the boats left the coast, Nedumaran sighed. He knew what was hidden inside those crates. The banned substances were shipped illegally from other countries and slipped into the hands of the criminals who distributed them to various dealers and who in turn would corrupt young minds. There were powerful forces backing the operation, so it would be futile for a single officer to stop these activities.

****

Jakarta, Indonesia

Madhirajan called his brother anxiously. How could they let that man walk out free? He had been charged with first degree murder as well as antiques smuggling. And he had been convicted for life.

He chewed his lips thoughtfully while he waited for his brother to answer the call.

"Hello Madhi?"

"Do you know that they are letting him out of the prison in two days?"

"Who?" Udayarajan asked in concern. The long-distance international call was feeble, but he could figure that his brother Madhirajan was perturbed.

"That fellow who arrived from Kuala Lumpur! What was his name? Oh yes Arumugam."

"What about him?"

"They are releasing him in two days."

"What? But was he not imprisoned for life?"

"Yes, he was! My sources tell me that his impeccable behaviour impressed the jailers and they recommended his name for early release."

"That is not what we want. What if he spills the truth about Raja Manickam?"

"Exactly. He might start talking about what he had learnt from our man during that journey from Kuala Lumpur to Chennai."

"Don't worry. I will take care of him."

"I wish I was there Uday. But you know we are on the verge of discovering the formulae for the ingredient."

"I know. Like I told you, he will not trouble us for long."

****

Neel entered the newly constructed arrival lounge of Anna International Airport. His tall build and brisk strides attracted attention, but Neel ignored it. He was fuming. The flight was already late by an hour and the flight attendant's inability to restrain his co-passenger who kept rambling in the craft after consuming a couple of glasses of whiskey annoyed him. He had no tolerance for fools.

The immigration formalities took a lot of time unnecessarily and he was almost on the verge of losing his temper at the officer. To top it all, the luggage took ages to reach. As he waited for his luggage near the carousal, he got an eerie feeling of being watched. He turned around to check if he knew any of the other passengers. No one looked familiar to him.

His friends had that wide-eyed look of wonder on observing an entirely new world and culture. He had not been keen on bringing Ann with him to India. He knew what his family would make of it, but she wanted to visit India, and this was as good a time as any to see the country. Rahul had an explanation for this; he said Ann was afraid that Neel's family would get him married off to some local lass. Neel sighed! Marriage or commitment to any relationship was the last thing on his mind now.

Balaji, the family driver glided in with the car, and he apologised profusely for having kept them waiting. Following in another car was his brother Mahesh and their family assistant. Mahesh jumped out and hugged him. Unlike Neel, Mahesh had no qualms about expressing his feelings physically or emotionally. For Neel such display of emotions was too personal.

"Hey bro, good to have you back."

"Yup, Mahesh this is Rahul, Mike and Ann. Guys this is my brother Mahesh."

"Neel, you didn't tell us you were bringing your girl-friend. Mom will be furious." Mahesh murmured to his brother in Tamil though he was awestruck by Ann's blonde hair and fair skin.

Neel shrugged, distracted by his interest in the blue Ferrari that his brother cruised in. It was a real beauty and he longed to take to its wheels. As soon as their luggage was loaded, he slid open the roof and zipped into the highway, heading towards the city.

Ann sat beside him and the other three followed him in another car. As he crossed the bridge over *Adyar* River, a bright hoarding flashed the family company's logo and the property that they had developed in the outskirts of the city.

****

In *Chidambaram Illam* the family awaited the boys' arrival eagerly. The *Puja* was over, and the family guru had retired to his abode. Arunachalam's sister Varalakshmy was visiting them with her family and staying over the night. She had a beautiful granddaughter, Shubashri who was in love with Nilagriva. Varalakshmy was aware of her granddaughter's feelings and she hoped to convince her brother of the alliance. She was confident that her brother would agree to it, but she was skeptical about Nilagriva's mother, Revathi. She didn't think that Revathi was keen on a union between Shubashri and Nilagriva. But Varalakshmy did not care about Revathi's acceptance or objection. After all, Nilagriva was going to be the next scion of the family business and he was handsome, intelligent and her brother's favourite. He reminded her of her brother Arunachalam in his younger days and Nilagriva had inherited the same arrogance and confidence from his grandfather.

Revathi awaited her son's arrival anxiously. It had been two years since she had seen Neel and she longed for a sight of him. The veranda where she was sitting with the others was long and winding. It divided the rest of the house from the garden and the porch. Her sisters-in-law were discussing the evil intentions of a character in their favourite television show and Revathi listened to them half-heartedly. A strange restlessness was bothering her. It was a well-lit night and the stars glowed across the sky brightly. A soft breeze was sweeping in from the garden carrying with it the smell of tropical flowers. Revathi inhaled the fragrance and closed her eyes assuring herself to stay calm. Her younger sister-in-law, Nalini noticed her worried face and reassured her,

"*Anni*, don't worry. Neel will be here soon."

Suddenly the car breezed in through the gates and came to a halt in the porch. Everyone stood up to welcome them. As Neel stepped out of the car, Ann opened the other door and climbed out of it. The family paused in a state of surprise and Nalini, who was always the first one to speak the obvious murmured, "*Anni,* you said he was bringing some friends, but he has brought an earthquake!"

The other car followed and soon Neel was introducing his friends to the family. Everyone sighed in relief as he introduced Ann as his friend. Neel was amused by his family's reaction. His aunts glared at Ann as if she belonged to another planet and his uncles looked confused. Thankfully, his brother and cousins made Ann and his friends welcome. He realised that to an outsider his family could seem daunting. He noticed his mother standing a little away and observing him. After he had greeted all, he approached her and smiled,

"Why are you standing so quietly here mom?"

His mother shook her head and replied, "I was yearning to see you and now that you are here, I don't know what to say."

"Mom, in my opinion you are the only one who knows to say the right things at the right time in this house," he teased her and draped his arm around her shoulders casually. His mother looked emotional and he was aware that she had missed him. She grinned at his compliment, grabbed his hands and led him to the kitchen. She opened a casserole and dished out a spoon of his favourite sweet. "Here taste this. I made it especially for you and before it gets wiped out, eat it first."

Neel tasted his favourite sweet and praised it. His tastes had changed over the years and it was no more his favourite sweet, but he did not let his mother know of it. He didn't want to hurt her feelings needlessly. He guided his mother back to the hall where everyone was chatting and laughing. Suddenly a hush fell on the room and he looked up the stairs to see his grandfather standing erect on the landing. Arunachalam climbed down the rest of the steps slowly and Neel realised that his hero, his mentor and his guide was not as agile as before. His grandfather had aged in the last couple of years. Neel rushed forward to meet him.

Arunachalam was overcome with emotions at the sight of his favourite grandson. There were so many unsaid things between them. For Arunachalam, it was like facing his own younger self. He could perceive the bottled-up emotions in his grandson. The silent guilt, the unjustified fury, the misunderstood accusation and the uncomfortable homecoming! Arunachalam clung to him in a tight embrace.

"Welcome home Nilagriva…."

Neel stiffened at the name. He stepped back from the embrace and stared at his grandfather who was an inch shorter than him. The lines of crease that fanned out on either side of his grandfather's face wrinkled into a frown and there were questions in his eyes as he regarded Neel.

"If the grand reunion between grandfather and grandson is over, shall we have dinner?" Neel's aunt demanded and everyone agreed.

Neel turned back but his grandfather stalled him, "Neel, who is that girl?"

"She is Ann, my friend and partner in the company. She wanted to tour India along with Rahul and Mike, so she accompanied us."

"Hmm…" Arunachalam held Neel's arm as he proceeded for dinner.

Neel's cousins surrounded him, and everyone wanted to know about his life in the U.S. There was good amount of teasing and bantering. As Revathi looked on, her eyes fell on her eldest sister-in-law Saraswathy. She was sitting quietly without indulging in any of the good-humoured discussions with a tight smile on her face. But a fleeting look in her eyes made Revathi uncomfortable. Since her son's death, Saraswathy had lost the joy and laughter in her life. Her husband had succumbed to a heart disease when her son Shreekant had been just six years old. Since then she had moved to *Chidambaram Illam* and took an active part in the running of the house. But her son's suicide had affected her gravely and she had sunk into depression, never recovering from the cruel blow. Sometimes, like today, when she looked at Neel, Revathi would catch a trace of anger and bitterness in her eyes which made her uneasy. It was difficult to perceive Saraswathy's feelings but Revathi's motherly instincts urged her to protect her son with a fervent need.

****

Jeeva signed the document and gave it to the officer. The policeman carried the document and proceeded towards the building that housed the cells. Jeeva waited anxiously for his uncle to be released from the prison. Twenty-four years ago, his uncle had been sent on an assignment from Kuala Lumpur to Chennai and it was here that he had been arrested. His uncle had been convicted for a crime that he insisted he hadn't committed but the law had found him guilty and had imprisoned him for life. But he would be released today and Jeeva had come from Fiji to take him home. Jeeva's mother had insisted that he bring his uncle to Fiji.

"Jeeva…"

He looked up and he was shocked to see his uncle frail and aged.

"Uncle, you look so worn out and exhausted."

"It has been twenty-four years Jeeva. How do you think I should look?" his uncle chided him and Jeeva collected the items that the jailer handed over to him. He took his uncle to the hotel he had booked for the night and explained about the journey back to Fiji to his uncle.

"No Jeeva, I am not coming to Fiji now." His uncle's words shocked him, and he asked, "But uncle why do you want to stay here? You don't know anyone here and this is not your home."

"Fiji is also not my home. I have to get back to Malaysia though nothing is left for me there. And I have some unfinished business here. "

"Uncle, you have a family in Fiji. You can stay with us. Mom is eagerly waiting

for you in Nadi."

"I know. Tell her I will visit her after I finish my work in Malaysia. You carry on."

Jeeva tried to convince his uncle to go back with him but he failed.

"Uncle, this place is dangerous for you. You said you were the victim of a conspiracy. What if the ones who conspired against you attacked you here?"

"Do not worry about me Jeeva. I am made of sterner stuff than you think."

The next day, Jeeva left for Fiji but he had no clue about his uncle's mission. He wondered what his uncle wanted to achieve by staying here and hoped that his uncle would return to Fiji safely.

****

At *Chidambaram Illam*, Neel Chandra stood outside his cousin Shreekant's room and closed his eyes. He had never entered the room after that fateful day, but he wanted to see it one last time before he left the country. He opened the bolt and entered the room tentatively. An eerie silence assailed him as he set foot inside the room.

5) THE FIRST CLASH

"Without praising you father; my days are unborn as you are the universe that encompasses the twinkling stars, the sky and all else." Thirumurai 6(1-4)

Neel looked around the room, trying to remember the happy times that he had spent with his cousin before his untimely death. Many times, he had come upon his cousin trying to inject himself with something and out of curiosity he had questioned him about it. But Shreekant had always dismissed him without any explanation. It was only later that he understood his cousin had a problem with substance abuse.

Memories did not allow Neel to stay in the room for long. He moved out hastily and on the way he came across the maid who gave him a thick envelope.

"What is this?"

"I don't know *anna*. The postman delivered it and Nalini *chithi* asked me to keep it in *appa's* room." She replied handing the envelope to Neel.

Neel looked at the envelope and checked the scrawled writing. It was addressed to his father. He headed to his parents' room, but his cell phone ring halted him. He strode quickly back to his room and answered the call. Ann reminded him about his plans for the day. Asking her to wait at the guest house, he tossed the packet on the bed and went down quickly to fetch his car.

****

Sindhoora rushed around the house in the morning hours. She was getting late for work and if she didn't reach on time, her boss would skin her alive. She could smell her mother's spicy *sambar*, could hear *Maharajapuram Santhanam's* rich and melodious voice from the stereo and the aroma of incense sticks wafted across the air. Her paternal grandmother Kalyani was chanting mantras engrossed in her own spiritual world. Her brother Adithya, who kept adjusting his spectacles to get a better look at the screen, was sprawled across the floor in the front room with his laptop, Physics book and assignments.

"Sindhu, will you be late tonight also?" Her mother yelled from the kitchen,

"Don't know *ma.*"

Her grandmother Kalyani muttered, *"Eppo parthalam oru arppattam! Ennathe kizhichirapore ippadi poradi?"* (Always demonstrating over something or the other…! What will you achieve by doing this?")

"Paati, there is always water crisis in the city. Instead of restoring the tank, they want to build a car parking. Is it fair? And after our demonstrations, the admin has promised to reconsider it," Sindhoora explained to her grandmother.

"Paati, she is Poet *Bharathiyar's* heroine…" Sindhoora's brother Adithya chipped in.

"Poda……"

Sindhoora was the darling of the family, and her brother Adithya always poked fun at her for it but he was her grandmother's favourite. Whatever be the situation, nobody could raise a voice against him in front of her grandmother. Sindhoora had complained about it to her parents sometimes, but Kalyani had grown up in an orthodox and conservative background and the mindset that put boys a notch above girls was deeply rooted in her. Nobody could alter her preconceived notions. When Sindhoora was young, her father had tried to pacify her by explaining about the problems that troubled *Paati* deeply. Kalyani had been cheated and thrown out of her family house in Coimbatore by her youngest son and she had been left to fend for herself. Her eldest son Vaidyanathan - Sindhoora's father, and Kalyani's daughter Usha had fetched her from the old -age home where her youngest son had abandoned her. As she grew older, Sindhoora learned to take *Paati's* taunts and bias in her strides. She also became aware of her father's financial worries. His job as a foreman in an Engineering unit did not earn him much and he had borrowed loans during her sister's marriage. He worried constantly about repaying these loans. So Sindhoora took up a job immediately after passing out of college. It has been six months since she took up the job. Her razor-sharp mind was adept at multi-tasking, so she was also preparing for Chartered Accountancy exams simultaneously. She did not wish to burden her father further with her own needs.

This morning was one of those bad days when nothing seemed to go right for Sindhoora. Her boss Mr. Pathi would give her an earful if she reached late; especially on this day when they were supposed to meet a new client. Pathi needed no reason to take her case and he waited for such opportunities eagerly. She has never figured out his contempt for her. Today, she missed the bus as she was late, so she hailed an auto. But the driver refused to run the meter box and locked horns with her all the way. She got so fed up of his argument that she threatened to take him to the police station. As soon as she uttered the word police, he stopped the auto midway and refused to go further. It was in the middle of a busy junction of the road and the traffic was at its peak. She signaled a traffic constable to help, even as a long queue of vehicles had formed behind the auto, honking and shouting at them to get moving. She stepped out of the auto to speak to the approaching traffic cop. The moment she stepped out of the auto; the rogue auto driver took off with his vehicle. The other cars and buses, waiting impatiently for the auto to move forward, followed the auto shortly. One of the oncoming cars would have hit her if the driver had not pulled the break in time. Furious at the foolish girl who was blocking the road, he got out of the car to check what the commotion was. Meanwhile, a state transport bus, surfacing suddenly from a blind alley hurtled towards them at speed. It would have hit both of them if he had not pushed her out-of-the-way and dragged her towards the footpath. The driver of the bus hurled abuses at her. Sindhoora pulled out of the arms that held her waist in a vice grip. She looked at her savior who was glaring as if she was a born imbecile.

She caught her breath at the furious face that was staring at her. The first thought that entered her head was the hostility that stemmed between them. His long straight hair that brushed his shoulder, his clenched strong jaw and his dark eyes stirred an instant aversion in her. She disliked his looks and hated his attitude. Yes, he had loads of attitude, almost as though he owned the road.

"Are you out of your mind? What were you doing in the middle of the road?" he barked at her. Sindhoora frowned. There was something different about his accent. She blinked at him.

The traffic constable joined them and berated her, "*ennama, nadu road le galatta pannreenga?*" (Why are you creating ruckus in the middle of the road?)

Her temper rose and she spoke sharply at him "I am causing trouble? If you had been strict with these auto fellows, they would not dare to be such hooligans. When it is compulsorily to use the meter, why are they not running it? How can they blatantly disregard the law?"

The man, who rescued her glanced at the traffic constable and then asked her, "Are you a social worker?" The constable laughed and shook his head. His question touched a raw nerve and she snapped at the stranger, "Don't dare to make fun of me." The man raised his eyebrow in scorn and giving her the once-over, he marched away. She turned towards the constable and rebuked him angrily, "And sir your job is to penalize the law-breaker and not stand here and share a joke."

"Don't teach me about my duties."

"Ok then, I will go to the press."

The word 'Press' impelled him into action, and he flicked out his pad, noting down the details of the disappearing auto. Sindhoora realised that one of her sandals had come out and she turned back to retrieve it. She observed the young man, who had rescued her out of the corner of her eye. He was sliding into his car. The constable stopped another auto and motioned the driver to take her to her destination. When Sindhoora climbed inside the auto, a blue Ferrari swept past it and she realised that it belonged to the stranger who had pulled her to safety. Sindhoora looked at the rear mirror of the auto and scowled at her reflection. Wisps of hair had come out of her single plait and her face looked plain and boring. But her eyes glittered with unexplained brightness. Sindhoora made a face at her reflection and brushed her tousled strands into place.

The day turned from bad to worse when she reached her office. Mr. Pathi had already left for his meeting with the new client and she waited tensely for his return. Her desktop computer gave trouble and it stopped working altogether after some time. She had to get the help of IT department to restart it. The moment her boss returned, he screamed at her for being careless and late. While her fellow workers sympathised with her, she had to work late in the evening and finish the presentation. Sindhoora worked for a firm that designed landscapes in the city. *'The Bay's Architects'* specialised in landscape architecture and ecological planning. She was training under various departments and her current assignment was in the accounts wing. She had to get the estimates from all departments, compile them and send it to the various administration managers who would, in turn, present it to the client.

As the late afternoon faded to early dusk, Sindhoora paused and checked the time. She sighed. She had another hour of work. Her stomach rumbled and she helped herself to a cup of hot coffee and a packet of chips. Her mind drifted to that morning when she had fought with the auto driver. Something about the incident bothered her. She could not point out exactly what it was that troubled her, but the more she tried to forget the incident, the more it disturbed her. Was it because the auto driver had fooled her and driven away or was it the haughty stranger who had saved her from an imminent danger? Instead of thanking him, she had taken an instant dislike to him.

That was it! She was annoyed because she did not thank him; instead she had snapped at him. Well, she didn't think he would have noticed her slip. He had been more interested in making fun of her.

Her mother telephoned her when she was about to leave the office. "Sindhu, *Paati* complained of chest pain and uneasiness in the evening. So, we are taking her to the hospital. Come straight to the hospital." Gayatri named the hospital and Sindhoora left her office in panic.

****

Ann was thrilled with the attention she got from Neel that day. On a joyride around the city, he showed her the longest coastline in the region and took her on a drive to the temple city of *Mahabalipuram*, situated on the southern coast of the Bay of Bengal. Neel did not know why he bothered to take so much trouble to make Ann happy. She was leaving for 'India Tour' in a couple of days and he would not be seeing her again till he went back to U.S. He had no plans to take her around the city when she had called him in the morning at his house. He had decided to meet her to wish her safe journey. But he changed his plan after the incident at the junction near *Chamiers Road* this morning. He was furious at the girl's stupidity. She should have been grateful that he had rescued her swiftly from approaching danger. But no, she had snarled at him like he was some interloper.

"Crazy woman!" He muttered.

"What? Did you say something Neel?" Ann who was enjoying the drive asked him.

"No nothing." He replied gritting his teeth at the irksome encounter. But he could not stop himself from recalling the moment when her eyes had roved around his face. Her dark eyes had spit fire at him. And he had also noticed her heart-shaped face and the wisps of hair that had come out of her plait. He hated girls who used their innocence to get attention. Like the girl who had deceived his cousin Shreekant. Damn! Where did that come from? He roused himself out of his wandering thoughts and lead Ann to the famed monuments.

By late evening, he dropped Ann at her hotel, and she invited him for a cup of coffee.

"Neel, when will you return to U.S?"

"Probably in a week's time…" He needed to speak to his family about his plans of continuing in the U.S.

"And then?" Ann asked him

"Then? What do you mean?"

"Where do I stand in your scheme of things Neel?" Ann asked as she handed him the cup of coffee.

"What do you mean where you stand? You have always known the score Ann. I haven't kept anything from you."

"I know Neel, but I want to settle down. And I love you. I can't think of anyone else with whom I would want to spend my life."

Neel's dilemma was obvious. He did not love her, but he liked her company. He did not want to hurt her, but he also wanted to be honest with her.

"Ann, I do not know what to say. You are beautiful, smart and you can get any guy you want."

"But not you?" Ann questioned him.

"No, I like you Ann but love? No, that is not possible." How could he let anyone know that he hated the feeling of being bound by emotions? Shreekant's death had put a seal on his emotions. "And you have known me for years Ann. Have I ever let you feel otherwise?"

Ann was quiet as she remembered all those days when they had fallen asleep in each other's arms. He had never confessed such feelings to her or anyone anytime, but she had hoped for a change of heart in him. She sighed wistfully and kissed him deeply.

"No, you have never, but I hope that you would miss me so much that all your theories would prove you wrong."

"Ann…" He tried to extricate himself from her embrace gently and left the room in haste.

While driving back, he decided to talk to his family about his plans for the future. He hoped that they would not be hurt by his intentions to settle abroad.

He reached home and decided to have a wash before dinner. As soon as he stepped inside, he saw the envelope that had arrived in the morning for his father. He picked up the packet and when he swung it, the flap of the envelope opened, and its contents spilled out.

He heard the clang of metal on the floor and bent down to inspect the contents. There was a small wrapped packet. He unfolded the sheet. A strange shaped key slipped from the sheet. He picked it up and studied it. *He had seen it before.* Then he read the words on the sheet. It was a couplet. There was another small note too and he read it with growing skepticism and bewilderment.

6) THE CRYPTIC MESSAGE

"Enchanted by the talks, he who stole my heart took a permanent place in my mind." Thirumurai 1(1-5)

Neel read the note with growing skepticism and bewilderment. A strange shaped key was wrapped in handmade paper and a couplet was written on it. The verse was beyond his comprehension. He read the lines once again,

"The King of the tongue was saved by the holy bull,

Even if he did a lot of misdeeds due to ignorance,

But your boy could not be saved by the evil pull,

That destroyed him due to their emergence…."

Frowning at the lines, Neel picked up the other sheet and read the hand-written note,

"The slave, troubled in mind, roaming around the ancient forests

Cradling the alms-bowl, craved for the poison…

Consumed by the fire with ignorance, descended down to the

End of the world, choking on struggling breath…."

The words were mystifying. Neel failed to decipher the meaning of the lines. It looked as if someone had taken great pleasure in penning down a few lines of an elegy. He studied the key. It was a small metallic strip of gold with a figure of an animal at the top. He pondered if it was a gift from some friend or client to his father. But the key did not seem new. It had rusted edges. In fact, it seemed to belong to a far-off period. Where had he seen the key before? Even if it was a gift, why would anyone send the morbid verses? He folded the sheets back into the envelope and placed the key carefully. He decided to give the confounding packet to his father.

He had covered half of the distance to the door of his room when something about the note and the key bothered him. He perused the lines once again and tried to recognise the words,

"The slave, troubled in mind, roaming around the ancient forests…"

Something about the word '*slave*' seemed familiar. He was not sure. And the key? Had he seen it somewhere?

He marched out of the room and came upon his father who seemed in a hurry. A handsome man in his late fifties, Chandra Shekhar was always engrossed in the functions of the company to the exclusion of other matters.

"Dad, this packet arrived for you in the post today. Sorry, I looked through the contents. They spilled out."

His father frowned at the packet, "Where is it from?"

Neel shrugged his shoulder and stood by to see his father's reaction as he unfolded the sheets from the envelope. Chandra Shekhar read the lines and studied the key. He turned the key over many times and inspected it.

"Whose key is it? And where did it appear from?" he asked Neel. He recited the verses and looked up in confusion, "Are these lines from some fancy fable?" Neel was amused at his father's disconcerted reaction.

"Dad, check the place from where it was posted." They examined the envelope and came upon the name of '*Cuddalore District*'.

"We have our business in the district, but the name of the town is unclear. I can't make it out. Keep it with you. We will identify the sender some other time. I am in a hurry. I have to go to Delhi early morning."

"Dad, I need to talk to you and mom about my plans for the future. Do you have time for it?" Neel asked as he remembered his earlier decision to talk to his family.

"Sorry Neel, not now. I will be back day after. We can discuss it then."

Neel watched his father as he strode out. He realised that the envelope remained in his hands and went back to his room to keep it in the sliding chamber of his closet. That night his friends, Rahul and Mike reminded him that their visit to the famous Lord *Shiva* temple was pending. Neel promised them that he would take them the next morning.

****

Sindhoora and her mother reached home late night. Akhil dropped them back from the hospital. Kalyani, Sindhoora's grandmother had suffered a mild heart attack and she was rushed to the hospital. The doctors had prescribed various tests to diagnose the exact cause for the attack. So, she was kept under observation at the hospital for the night.

Next morning, Sindhoora's mother Gayatri asked her to visit their neighborhood temple with the garland she had made for the deity. Kalyani never missed a single day to offer the garland in the temple. Now that she was in the hospital, her daughter-in-law did not want to discontinue the customary offering. When Akhil's mother arrived with food that she had cooked for the family, she accompanied

Sindhoora to the temple.

Being a Monday, there was a long queue at the Shiva temple and Sindhoora along with her aunt followed the queue which moved at a very slow pace. Sindhoora became a little impatient as she had to leave for work soon. If she did not reach office on time that morning, she concluded that Mr. Pathi would dismiss her with utmost glee. The *Kodimaram* glittered in the sun and Sindhoora regarded the shining flag post, noticing the birds perched at the top.

This was the most famous *Shaivite* temple in the city and it had visitors from all over the world. There was a golden *Gopuram* (monumental tower) and exquisite sculptures of different Hindu gods to worship. There were also idols of 63 *Nayanars* inside the main shrine. The *Nayanars* were a group of saints who lived in 6th to 8th century devoted to Lord Shiva.

Most of the devotees standing in the line carried some offering for the deity. The garland Sindhoora brought was made of *Vilvam* leaves known to be dear to Lord Shiva. Sindhoora was studying the shape of leaves when their queue paused without moving ahead. An administrative official ushered a small group of tourists into the *Mandapam* bypassing the queue. Sindhoora's temper rose and some of the devotees standing in the line complained about the unfairness of it.

One of them said, "Why don't they let the tourists visit at a different hour? This is so biased." And another replied in annoyance, "We people forget our own natives when we see foreigners..."

Sindhoora paid scant attention to their grievances but she viewed the tourists with resentment for delaying her. There was a pair consisting of a young fair woman and a man, along with two other men. The other two men seemed to belong to the city, but the one with a tiny ponytail attracted her attention. Sindhoora could see his tapering back in white linen shirt and blue jeans. His ponytail reminded her inadvertently of the stranger who had rescued her the previous day. Did every guy sport long hair these days? She wondered sardonically. He had draped one arm protectively around the tall and slender woman's waist as if she would get lost in the milieu. The group moved into the main hall and Sindhoora lost sight of them as she waited at the open yard in front of the golden *kodi maram* in the queue.

When the group came out of the hall, the queue started moving ahead, she muttered to her aunt, "This happens only in India. We become insignificant as soon as these outsiders throw their weight around."

She didn't care that the group, standing close to her across the rope that separated the line from others, could hear her. The tall man in the ponytail turned around swiftly and stared at her. His eyes narrowed in recognition. She was startled to find the same striking face that had rebuked her for standing in the middle of the road on the previous day. She was taken aback by his words next.

"Who became insignificant?" he asked her. So, he understood her mother tongue since her conversation with her aunt was in Tamil.

"I wasn't speaking to you," she replied curtly, and he raised his eyebrows, "No? I thought you said you had become insignificant."

"So? I was speaking to my aunt. Do you eavesdrop on everyone?" she asked rudely. Her aunt tugged her sleeve and gestured her to behave properly.

"No not everyone but I, sure as hell, do eavesdrop on the ungrateful ones who can't take their eyes off me," he answered in a clipped voice and those standing nearby heard him. They looked at her with amusement. Sindhoora had difficulty in holding back the fury that was sweeping over her. She wanted to scream indignantly at his audacity.

His friends, who had walked ahead, heard the mild commotion and approached him to enquire about it. The fair woman nudged him and tried to pull him away. Sindhoora was so provoked that she could not keep silent. Her aunt tried to drag her, but she resisted. She looked at his woman friend and asked her, "Why don't you ask your punk to behave himself? He seems to think no end of himself, as though he is a rock star."

Sindhoora spoke each word clearly and loudly. Then pretending to dismiss him and his friends as waste of time, she moved ahead without looking back at them. Her aunt rendered an angry glance at her. Other devotees smirked at him and strode ahead, forgetting the incident.

Ann could not resist grinning at Neel's infuriated expression. Repeating the girl's words, *my punk* she burst out laughing. Neel lost sight of the impertinent girl as the devotees entered the main shrine. Ann dragged him away from the hall and exited the temple porch.

She shared the joke with Rahul and Mike. "Seriously? She called him punk?" Mike asked and Rahul continued the bantering, "Whoa, I want to see her."

"But Neel what did you tell her that provoked her so much?" Ann asked him as she recollected the girl's angry face.

Neel shrugged, "Forget it. I don't remember. Let us leave guys. It is time to visit the consulate."

****

Sindhoora's aunt chastised her for being rude and audacious to a stranger. "Sindhu, you must be more careful while talking to strangers. We don't know what type of people we are dealing with. And these days, you can never predict what they would do next."

Her aunt continued with her censuring and Sindhoora heard her out without any argument. As they circumambulated the temple, his words, "*…to ungrateful ones who can't take their eyes off me*" resonated in her ears. So, he did take note that she had not thanked him for his help the previous day.

As soon as Sindhoora and her aunt left the temple layout, it started drizzling. There was a row of cars waiting on the narrow road near the tank to exit for the main road. But not a single *rikshaw* or *auto* was in sight. They started walking home. The city was gearing itself for the harvest festival, *Thai Pongal* but the unseasonal showers dampened the festive spirits. They did not carry an umbrella so Sindhoora covered her head with her *dupatta* and they quickened their pace to avoid getting too wet.

****

Neel, who waited impatiently in the car with his friends for the traffic mess to clear out, spotted her and her older companion striding without an umbrella. He took note of the way she let her stole cover her head. His friends were busy making plans in the car for their last night in the city and they demanded a party from him. They called up his brother to arrange for it. Neel listened to them in vague distraction. His attention was riveted on the girl. There was something about her that tugged his interest. The cars inched forward and he saw her at the end of the road trying to cross it. She scanned both sides of the road, took the older woman's arm and guided her to the other side of the road. Then she vanished from sight. Neel's eyes searched every corner of the road, but he could not find them. Then it was time for him to drive away from the locality. And he pushed the girl's image out of his head deliberately.

****

The party at the affluent pub of the luxurious hotel went on till wee hours of the morning. Neel's friends, brother and cousins danced away the night merrily without a care. One of his cousins tried to flirt with Ann but she paid no attention to him. Her focus was on Neel Chandra. She persuaded Neel to the dance floor and she casually brushed her arms against his, pulled him closer, making him sway in tune with her own motion, encircling him with her arms, while trying to whisper something into his ears. But it seems Neel existed in a realm beyond the reach of her sexual overtures, as if he was thwarting all her desperate efforts to win him over. His disinterest was not lost on Shubashri who was also present at the party. She got a vicarious pleasure from watching his aloofness and indifference, thrilled that Neel did not reciprocate the affections that Ann displayed publicly.

Neel asked for his favourite brand of beer and settled on the bar stool with his drink. He was relieved to be left alone finally. A middle-aged man joined him on the next seat and with a friendly smile; he toasted his drink, "Cheers!"

Neel followed the stranger's high spirits and raised his own glass in toast.

"Hi, Arumugam…." He introduced himself.

"Neel" he did not elaborate although the man wanted him to say more.

"That is quite a party you are having," He added

Neel smiled but remained quiet. The stranger concentrated on his own drink and left the bar after a couple of pints.

Suddenly Neel heard screams and the party ground to a sudden halt. Neel watched with dismay as the man called Arumugam collapsed on the floor near the doorway. When Neel rushed to him, the man was already dead.

7) THE MYSTIFYING DEATH

"Drawn to you, you prevailed over me; lucky are those, who with their insight feel your divine presence." Thirumurai 8 (1-1)

Neel was dismayed to see the man called Arumugam collapse on the floor. He rushed toward him and asked the bartender to get water. By the time, the glass of water was brought, the man had stopped breathing. Neel checked his pulses while his cousins and friends peered at the man apprehensively. The manager of the pub called the ambulance service and the party wound up. Neel asked his cousins to leave the premises and he asked his brother to escort Mike and Ann home. Neel and Rahul stayed back in the pub to aid the manager. They followed the ambulance in their car and the doctor at the Emergency declared the man dead. Cardiac arrest was stated as the cause of death. The police arrived and questioned Neel. The man's family needed to be informed, so the quest for his identification began. The Police shared his photograph on social media and informed relevant sources. Except for a wallet that had a few notes of Indian currency, there was nothing that identified him. Neel waited at the hospital for some bit of information on the man. There was a touch of remorse in him for not responding to the friendly advances of Arumugam at the bar.

One of the police constables received a message from another police station. Arumugam was apparently imprisoned for many years and he was released only two days ago. Neel was aghast. So, the man was a criminal, but he did not look like one. But then how did a criminal look? He asked himself ambiguously.

By morning, the man's nephew who resided in Fiji was informed and with his permission, the body was sent for post-mortem.

****

When dawn broke across the rolling hills, Ponmalan was already in his farm checking the effects of the new pesticide he had sprayed on the shrubs. The early morning telephone call woke him. Nothing was going right for him these days. Why these days? Nothing had been going right for him for many years now. Since he'd killed that rich boy in the city, there had been only mishaps in his life. Or was it because of the loss of the talisman that he had always worn around his neck? His father had gifted him the key and he had asked Ponmalan to treasure it. But he had lost it years ago because of the junkie called Shreekant. Now his father was dead, and his wife had left him for another man in the city.

Ponmalan's ancestor Meymaran had been a trusted servant of a sentinel in Chidambaram and he was asked to treasure a sacred key, believed to bring luck to the family. He left Chidambaram due to an emergency. Following the coastline, he travelled from Chidambaram to Kancheepuram. The city built by the *Pallavas* had stunned him and the famous *Ekambereshwar* temple in Kancheepuram, rebuilt by *Chola* Kings had fascinated him. The temple, where the lord resided in the form of *Prithvi*, one of the five elements, had many legends to tell its visitors. Meymaran earned his income by reciting the ancient verses that he had learnt in Chidambaram and entertained the visitors by narrating the folklore of the renowned temple. He settled down in one of the villages and his children continued the tradition of storytelling. Over the years, the key was passed from one generation to the next and through the years, the family preserved it with utmost care. Storytelling did not fetch much of an income; so, the later generations of the family faced abject poverty and famine. One of the descendants of Meymaran married a woman belonging to the *Irulla* tribe while travelling to *Nilgiris* and he settled down with her in the valleys of the *Nilgiris*. With the wife's expertise, the family brewed medicines and healed the villagers. The later generations veered towards mixing potent concoctions with herbs for sheer pleasure of the senses and earned money doing that. When illicit drugs were prohibited, they prepared mixtures clandestinely for a reserved set of clientele. The fabled key was treasured as a prized possession in the family.

Ponmalan had worn the key around his neck as a locket but one day it got lost while selling his drugs. He realised that Shreekant had stolen it from him and he had set out to retrieve the key. But he had ended up killing Shreekant. And the key was gone forever.

Now he lived alone, fending for himself by putting up a tea stall at the *'Flower Valley'* station (a hamlet in the *Nilgiris* valley). Only two trains passed through the station during the day and his stall was the only one which served tea to them. No one else dared to compete with him in the tiny hamlet. Children feared him because he was not pleasant to look at. The deep gash across his jaw gave him a sinister appearance. The men were wary of him because in the deep gorge of the *Nilgiris,* the whisper of the wind carried the hearsay that Ponmalan killed his own father. The women dismissed him because he could not even take care of his wife who had left him for another man. So Ponmalan grew his own herbs, brewed his own drinks with produce from his farm and his isolated existence went unnoticed by the law.

The early morning phone call had disturbed him. He was summoned by the man, who had bailed him out from the clutches of law once, to stalk the young scion of the same family. If Ponmalan visited them again, would he be able to retrieve his key? Ponmalan was convinced that his fortune may change for the better once he had the key back in his possession.

****

Sindhoora could not stop thinking about her confrontation with the group of tourists in the temple. Her aunt described the incident to every member of the family who visited her grandmother Kalyani. And each one of them berated her for her impudence. The incident distressed even her cousin Akhil.

"Sindhu, why did you engage in a fight at the temple? *Amma* has been so worried about it," he demanded fretting, while they were sitting outside Kalyani's ward in the hospital the next morning.

"Oh, stop it Akhil. I don't understand why *athai* is making such a fuss about it. It was just an exchange of harsh words. Nothing happened really." Her aunt's constant sermon about the episode exasperated Sindhoora. She wanted to forget it, especially the long-haired man whose face kept intruding into her thoughts at odd hours of the day.

"But Sindhu, what if he had accosted you on the road for being rude to him? What then?"

"Akhil for god's sake, he is not the type," she blurted out.

"How do you know his type? This was the first time you were meeting him."

Akhil's never-ending interrogation annoyed her. Sindhoora held back from explaining about their earlier clash on the road. Akhil would then start to lecture her on road safety.

"No, I have not met him and Akhil, will you stop irritating me with your questions?"

"Oh! So now I always irritate you with my attitude. You never seem to understand that I am concerned, and I worry about your safety."

"Relax Akhil, you are not my father," Sindhoora chided him, not realising that he was hurt by her rebuke. He fell silent. When there was no response, Sindhoora regarded his hurt expression and apologised. She touched his shoulder, "Akhil, I am sorry. It is just that everyone is making a mountain out of a molehill."

Akhil stood up abruptly and stepped away from her. He looked perturbed. Sindhoora noticed his tense face and asked him, "Akhil what is the matter? Why are you so disturbed?"

"You don't understand Sindhu. You never get it."

Startled by his impassioned plea, Sindhoora noticed that he avoided her eyes.

"What do I not understand Akhil?" she asked him hesitatingly, registering the restlessness in him. A sixth sense warned her that this moment was going to change their friendship forever.

Akhil knelt in front of her and took her palms in his. Frowning at him, Sindhoora checked if anyone was present at the corridor of the hospital. There was no one except for a nurse who was talking with a relative of another patient.

"I love you Sindhu. I have been in love with you for ages." Lifting her hands, he brushed his lips on the soft inner skin of her palms.

Shocked beyond words, she jerked her hands out of his grip and stood up angrily. She had never suspected his feelings for her. At a loss for words, Sindhoora was unable to respond to him. Overshadowing everything was her embarrassment at his confession. Akhil rose up slowly and faced her in nervous anxiety. Sindhoora could not meet his eyes. She stomped out of the corridor as he called out her name.

She met her father on the way and told him that she was going to office. Her grandmother would be discharged from the hospital that morning, so she did not have a reason to hang around the hospital. She took a city bus from the hospital and travelled to her workplace in a troubled state of mind. She could not erase from her mind the unconcealed desire that she found in Akhil's eyes while, he confessed his love. It disturbed and jolted her out of the complacent state that she had slipped into.   Even though she was aware that men found her attractive sometimes, she had no indication about Akhil's feelings. And had it been someone else other than her cousin, she would have perhaps reciprocated the feelings. But she had never thought of Akhil that way. She wanted to flee and cuddle inside her mother's protective cocoon. Distressed that Akhil's feelings had disturbed the innocence of their relationship, she also realised that her affections for her best friend were akin to the ones she felt for her brother, Adithya.

In the evening, her friend Vidya called her, "Sindhu, I have an extra pass for the concert. It is the last one for the season. Why don't you come? It is one of your favourite artists."

"When is it?"

"Tonight. If you leave the office now, you can reach the auditorium in time."

"Ok. I will talk to dad and let you know." Sindhoora wanted to attend the concert. The performer was her favourite violinist and they had missed the opportunity last time because of their inability to obtain the expensive tickets. The costs of tickets for these concerts were high during the season and one could avail them only if one was a member of the academy or was affluent enough to buy it in advance.

She sought her father's permission and left the office happily to enjoy a few hours of Carnatic music. And the uppermost thought in her mind was that she didn't have to meet Akhil. She was not an escapist, but till date she had been ignorant when it came to matters of the heart. Hence, she wanted to be certain of her response before she met him next.

****

Mrs. Revathi Chandra Shekhar took the most comfortable seat in the auditorium. The acoustics in the auditorium were one of the finest and she looked forward to a few hours of uninterrupted music. Music always soothed her nerves and she loved this distinct form of music that she was well versed with. She always attended these concerts alone, unmindful of her solo appearance. Her eyes appraised the dimly lit hall. She found couples, friends and family huddled together discussing the merits and demerits of the concerts of the current season. She would have loved to be part of such analysis, but she felt unwelcome. Though she belonged to one of the affluent families in the city, sometimes she keenly experienced this sense of being an outsider, as if somehow she did not possess the elite pedigree that qualified her to be part of the fraternity of Carnatic music connoisseurs, as if merely being able to enjoy the music was not enough. Sometimes she envied that aura of exclusivity that emanated from those patrons of the music. And it could be her fanciful imagination, but sometimes she also sensed a class bias that extended to even avid listeners like her. Of course, she was not averse to admitting that she had her own share of snobbery, perhaps a kind of inverse snobbery, which looked down upon some of those regular patrons of the art, those who belonged to the so-called exclusive community. She was also aware of the debates raging in the music circles over the unconventional approaches practised by some of the more radical new artists. But she admired the fact that despite the new trends, the opposing views and the conflicts, the rich heritage of this music continued to be revered and savoured. She however wished that there was someone in the family with whom she could share the pleasure she got from the music. She was married at a young age into the family of Arunachalam Chettiar, whose forefathers were traders. Over the years they had built up a conglomeration of companies and business. Money, finance and business ran in their blood. They considered art of any form as the pursuits of the affluent and aristocratic. But her mother-in-law changed their perceptions. She encouraged Revathi to pursue her hobby and attend concerts. But now that her mother-in-law was no more, she felt bereft of companionship.

As the auditorium filled up, she felt a strange uneasiness in her chest. It has been troubling her for some days and each time she dismissed it as a momentary soreness. She took a deep breath and waited for the pain to ease out. Then she settled down to enjoy the performance.

****

Sindhoora and her friend sat in one of the last rows. During a brief and uncustomary break, Sindhoora and Vidya went out to buy some snacks from the canteen and discussed certain ragas and compositions. Sindhoora did not check her phone. She was still unprepared to speak to Akhil. The interval came to an end and the listeners surged back to the hall. Vidya advanced to the counter to pay the bill. It was then that Sindhoora noticed the woman clutching the handle of the washroom door tightly. She seemed anxious and disturbed. Sindhoora delivered the plate on the counter and dashed to help the woman.

8) THE ACCIDENTAL CONFRONTATION

"The swelling waters that meet the shellfish on the sands of the shore," Thirumurai 2 (1-2)

Neel reached home after dropping his friends at the airport. He went straight to his room to have a wash.

His cell phone vibrated. It was his mother.

"Hello, Mom?" But it was not his mother's voice at the other end.

"No, this is not your mother. We are at Trithya Sangeet auditorium. Your mother fell unconscious."

"What?"

"She is fine now. She asked us to call you."

"Wait. I am coming. Please stay with her. I will reach in ten minutes."

"Sure, we will wait."

"Thanks"

Neel sped out of the house without noticing the car that tailed him.

****

Sometimes life indeed was stranger than fiction, but then nothing ever happened by chance either. These thoughts swept through Neel's head as he entered the auditorium complex. For, he saw her standing next to his mother sharing a comfortable rapport. Stepping out of the car angrily he approached them in resentment.

"Sindhoora, look at that guy. He is so sexy!" Vidya exclaimed very softly and Sindhoora who was chatting with the woman looked up. Taking a second look at the man striding towards them, she stared at him in astonishment. What was happening in her life? From somewhere, a quote surfaced in her mind, its words jogging her memory, *"We don't meet people by accident. They are meant to cross our path for a reason."*

What was the long-haired man doing here? Earlier, when she noticed the woman clutching the door of the washroom, she had rushed forward to help her. The woman had almost passed out when Sindhoora reached her. With Vidya's help, she had supported the woman before she slumped down completely. They had made her sit on the chair and fetched her a glass of water. She had looked stressed out. After making sure that she was alright, Sindhoora volunteered to take her home. It was then that the woman requested Sindhoora to contact her son, Neel. Waiting for her son to arrive, they gave her company till then. Little did she expect that she would be coming across the same snooty man third time in a row.

Neel reached them and exclaimed in anger, "You!" and added, "Are you following me?"

Sindhoora looked at him indignantly wanting to swear at his arrogance.

"Do you know each other?" Revathi glanced at both of them and asked in surprise.

"No"

"Yes"

While Neel admitted to meeting her, Sindhoora denied and an amused Revathi quipped, "Either you know each other, or you don't. And Neel…. she was the one who contacted you," she explained to her son.

"Oh…"

"Yes, and contrary to your assumptions, I have better things to do in life than follow you," Sindhoora's retort astounded her friend Vidya. She stared at Sindhoora with interest.

Neel ignored her and looked at his mother, "Are you alright now?" When his mother tried to rise from the chair, Neel helped her by holding her shoulders gently. From a cold and arrogant stranger to a perfect gentleman with his mother, his transformation surprised Sindhoora. His mane of shoulder-length hair was open, and he wore a light jacket over his shirt and trouser. When he straightened, he caught Sindhoora staring at him and raised an eyebrow wryly at her. Embarrassed, she cursed herself for being stupid. When she turned around to go back to the auditorium, the woman's voice halted her.

"Sindhoora…"

"Thank you for helping me. Neel will drop you back home. The concert is almost over."

Sindhoora could sense Neel's irritation at his mother's invitation.

"Thanks aunty but we will take an auto."

"No Sindhoora. It is quite late. Come, we will drop you home. Won't you Neel?" She appealed to her son who was getting increasingly annoyed. He shrugged in indifference while his eyes gleamed with anger.

"I will get the car."

The powerful and sleek car cruised smoothly and halted beside them. Neel helped his mother to the front seat while Revathi urged Sindhoora and Vidya to get inside the car. Sindhoora hesitated and looked at Vidya who had no qualms about accepting the comfortable ride. She settled into the seat without giving it much thought. Sindhoora stood holding the door warily.

Neel observed Sindhoora's dilemma and held the door open for her. She swung around to face him, and his eyes bore into hers. He held her gaze and she could not look away. A tension gripped them. This time there was no hostility, no anger, just an intense awareness of each other. From inside the auditorium, the last notes of the *Ragam-Tanam-Pallavi* reached a crescendo followed by thundering applause. Sindhoora became aware of her surrounding and let herself into the car hastily as Neel shut the door.

During the drive, Neel ignored both the girls except to ask for directions to their house. He was more concerned about his mother as Revathi explained about the frequent pains that assailed her in recent days. Neel booked an appointment with the doctor for his mother next day as the car sped along *Royapettah* towards *Mylapore*.

The car tailing them at a distance was inconspicuous in appearance and the man inside the car frowned at the route that Nilagriva Chandra Shekhar took. This was not the route they had come by. And while he had waited outside the auditorium for Neel to reappear, he had set the map back for the location of his house. But now he was confused. Still the man followed the car.

Sindhoora was not ashamed of her middle-class upbringing or her background but when the elegant car came to a halt in front of the street of her house, she wished for a moment that the area was not as shabby as it looked. The car could not enter her street as it was too narrow and there were two cars parked already in front of other houses. So, Neel dropped her at the end of the street and Revathi thanked her once more for her help. Sindhoora noted that Neel did not even have the courtesy to turn and look at her. He drummed his fingers impatiently on the steering wheel waiting for his mother to end her conversation.

"Thankless fellow, ungrateful man…." Sindhoora groused loudly as she and Vidya strode along the remaining stretch of the road.

"Sindhu, what are you muttering?"

"Nothing! Just calling him names!"

"Who? Neel? He was so good-looking," Vidya voiced her appreciation and glared at Sindhoora, "By the way Sindhu, you didn't tell me that you have met him before. How mean!"

"I haven't met him. We just got into an argument at the temple the other day over his breaking the queue. That is all." She chose to omit their first meeting.

"Oh!"

They reached home and Sindhoora was relieved that Akhil was not present at home. While she got ready for bed, she thought over the eventful day. First, Akhil's confession at the hospital, then her confrontation with Neel! The momentary spell between them etched in her mind like a mysterious stone marker. A tremor went through her as she recollected the instance. She was enraptured by his velvet-black eyes that had smoldered at her with their intensity. She could have lost herself under his spell. She shivered at the thought. What was happening to her? And suddenly the contrast in her feelings hit her hard. There was none of that aversion that she felt for Akhil, when he had bared his feelings to her that morning.

Instead, here there was curious fascination. The reason she concluded was that instead of desire, she had seen derision in Neel's eyes. He had dented her ego and maybe that is the reason he intrigued her. No man had looked at her with such disdain and scorn. But she had liked his mother. She was a lovely, soft-spoken woman. Unlike her son! She reflected with a sigh. She hoped that the doctor would not diagnose anything serious with Neel's mother.

****

Neel accompanied his mother to the doctor next day and after his examination, the doctor advised her to take things easy. He prescribed medicines for hypertension. While driving back home, Neel counselled his mother on her health,

"Mom, you must take things easy. There are others in the family to take care of the running of the house. Why do you always end up with the entire responsibility?"

"It has become a habit Neel. I don't know what I would do if I didn't have the household chores to complete. Your father is never at home. You are not living here, and you have no interest to stay at home. Mahesh is always busy. What would I do? The only thing I love is music."

Neel frowned at his mother's words. He had not realised that his mother felt so forlorn at home. He had always been under the impression that his mother loved being the homemaker.

"I was not aware that you felt so alone mom," Neel admitted.

"I know Neel. You had your own demons to deal with." Revathi learnt long ago that Neel had been nursing an inner guilt ever since his cousin died.

"Mom, you should speak to dad. Maybe that will help. Why don't you go on a holiday with him?"

Revathi laughed sardonically at her son's suggestion, "Do you know how much I had wanted to visit you the last three years? Every time I raised the topic, your father would get annoyed and remind me of the huge responsibility that he was shouldering. I stopped suggesting vacations to him finally."

Neel was startled to know that his mother had wanted to visit him during the last three years. He glanced at his mother's face as she leaned her head on the back rest. There was exhaustion and fatigue stamped on her face. The ends of her tresses had turned grey and he realised that she had neglected herself over the years. But she still looked lovely. His father had once told him that she was the loveliest woman he had ever seen and that he had fallen in love with her the moment he saw her holding the tray of coffee at her house in Madurai.

So, what happened to the romance between his parents? He asked himself. Why was his father so busy when he had his brothers and cousins to delegate the workload? Did his absence create a rift between them?

"I think I blamed him in my own way for sending you away from home all those years ago," Revathi spoke softly and Neel was taken aback. "What about dad? How did he feel?" Neel asked his mother as thoughts of his father propelled him to question. Did his father too feel lonely?

"I don't know. We hardly speak to each other now. He is too busy with his work and I get too exhausted when he reaches home."

"Mom, you should take up some hobby to de-stress."

"I know. I should have pursued music, but after your grandmother's death there was no one to encourage me. And I just gave up on it."

"Why do you need someone to encourage you? If music interests you, pursue it. "

"Neel, everyone needs constant motivation in his or her life. There are very few people who follow their heart without another's influence. I admire such people, but I am not one of them."

Neel was suddenly accosted by the image of Sindhoora. He didn't think she would need anyone's encouragement to pursue what she wanted to do. He guessed that if she set her heart on something, she would definitely do it. The haphazard thoughts disturbed him. She seemed to appear in his head every couple of hours and every time he tried to erase her image, it only strengthened its hold on him.

"I really enjoyed the first half of the session last night. The performance was amazing. Even Sindhoora loved the concert." Neel was speechless at the way his mother spoke her name with such ease.

He was silent. He wished that his mother would stop talking about the girl who seemed to have taken a permanent place in their thoughts.

****

Nedumaran paced up and down the coastline in restlessness. Feeling weary with exertion, he rested his aged body on the secluded shore sometime later and watched the dancing sea. Like him, the ultramarine water seemed disordered today. The blue-gray waves dashing against the beach sprayed him with their salty showers and left remnants ashore like their blessings on the continuous piece of land. He surveyed the residue with a sigh. With another leap from the ocean, they would be taken back to the same spot from where they had arrived. The abysmal sea loved to play this game of hide and seek with its possessions. He observed the shell of a crab that was carried ashore by the wave. And within a minute, the shell was fetched back into the swirling water by another giant wave. Nedumaran grinned at the playfulness of the ocean. It seemed to take great pleasure in performing like an acrobat with its belongings.

He lay down on the beach and closed his eyes listening to the thundering sounds of the ocean. He wished the sea would swallow him and end his journey on earth. He did not wish to live anymore but he reasoned that if he was still alive, then there was perhaps an impending mission, waiting for him. Like the *Irulla* tribes of *Pichavaram* mangroves that seemed to have existed from time immemorial, he seemed to have stayed on the earth forever. He had inferred that by posting the message and sending it to the address, his obligation to the family was over. But it had been a week since he had sent it and there has been no word from them. He was not even sure if they had received it. He contemplated travelling to Chennai to meet the family.

He snapped out of his trance, to glimpse a streak of lightening across the darkening sky. The harvest festival was round the corner and the brightest star would resume its brilliance to give life to the colorless and insipid. The forthcoming festival reminded him of her lovely face and gentle voice and his devotion to her was as pure as the winds of the Thillai Forests.

9) JEEVA VELU STANE

"*Your aroma is omnipresent like you…*"   ***Thirumurai 8 (1-1)***

Nedumaran met her for the first time when she had come to Chidambaram for a visit as a young bride during the harvest festival many years ago. He had already lived three and half decades in the sublunary world and being a cynic, he did not expect the ethereal intervention at that juncture in his life. She had been very young and lovely, but it was only when she started to sing at the shrine that she captivated him. He had made a sojourn to the *Nataraja* temple to deliver the sack of coconuts from *Killai* orchard. And on his way to the kitchen, he had heard the silvery voice that carried melodious tunes in praise of the Lord. He had halted at the doorway to listen to her and it was the first time that he saw her. One can assume that Nedumaran was well and truly bewitched. Her eyes were closed in concentration and she had not been aware of anyone but the lord. Her devotion to the art and the purity in her voice had enslaved him to her for eternity. But neither did she see him then nor was she ever aware of his existence. When she belted out the last notes of the song, her young husband had come back to take her with him. And it was the last time that Nedumaran got to behold the sight of that lovely face.

The memories dimmed when he heard the Rain God vying to make his presence with thunder and lightning. He scowled at the unseasonal and ominous clouds. Why was there a change in the elements of nature? Did they signify the harbinger of a new era? Nedumaran pondered as he stroked his long beard and strolled back to his house slowly.

****

In Chennai, the police officers could not explain the chain of events

91

leading to his uncle's cardiac arrest. They advised Jeeva to speak to Neel Chandra.

When Neel returned home with his mother after the medical consultation, a visit from Arumugam's nephew surprised him. Neel found an attractive young man around his own age in casual attire. His clean-shaven face, short blunt hair and tattooed arms with oriental script and designs implied contradicting traits of a personality. While the other man's light eyes studied him curiously, Neel noticed the odd piece of jewelry that adorned a single ear.

"Hi, Neel Chandra"

"Jeeva" They shook hands, appraising each other cautiously.

****

The conference room was packed with their employees and everyone paid attention to the speaker who was addressing them from the podium.

"So, you have to pause and listen to the land that you are standing upon. It is not just the client that we should interest in pleasing. The land also matters. We have to please the land as much as our client. And it is the one which has sustained us for years…"

In spite of her lack of knowledge in the subject, Sindhoora was spell-bound by the speaker's chalk talk. There was a seminar in the office for the staff and one of the leading landscape architects in the country was giving a discourse on developing landscapes. He specialised in sustainable landscapes, having been in the business for more than fifteen years in India and other countries. Though Sindhoora initially attended the seminar because it was mandatory for all employees, her interest and attention were soon captured by the lecture.

"Sometimes you find infinite silence in the valley and sometimes you can hear the hum of a trickling stream and sometimes the whisper of the wind. The land is speaking to you in its own ways. Do not try to overwhelm it with great designs and huge ambitions. Listen to them and work around in amicable ways to magnify their appeal. You can't drive out a rare species to build a park for us to enjoy. That disturbs the balance of the natural eco system...."

Sindhoora could have gone on listening to him for days. The subject was fascinating, and she had never thought of land as a living entity. His words stressed on the need to not take the planet for granted. He continued to explain that every piece of land held untold treasures and it was the duty of every person to explore them and preserve them before building opulent structures rampantly.

Sindhoora made a special note to focus on the nature of the work of the firm she was working for and learn about their approach and techniques.

****

At *Chidambaram Illam*, Neel extended his condolences to Jeeva on his uncle's demise.

"Sorry about your uncle."

Jeeva nodded, letting his eyes roam around the house before mentioning, "I heard that you were present when he collapsed."

"Yes, I was at the pub that night. In fact, a bunch of us were partying. Your uncle arrived late, and we exchanged small talk. And it was while he was leaving that he suffered the heart attack. Have you received the post-mortem report?"

"No, I was informed that it would take a couple of days more." Jeeva continued, "There is a funeral service for him at an address that the embassy gave. It is on Thursday. Do come."

"Sure." They skirted around the topic of Arumugam because neither was too sure of how to kick-start the conversation. Jeeva was uncertain about Neel's knowledge of his uncle's imprisonment, while Neel pondered about the offense that Jeeva's uncle had committed.

Neel could perceive that Jeeva was reluctant to talk about his uncle, so he asked him about his life in Fiji and he was surprised to know that Jeeva worked as a disc jockey during weekends and managed a small banana plantation rest of the time. Neel had not visited Fiji though he had been to Tonga, one of the islands nearest to Fiji.

"Where are you staying here?"

"Hotel South Residency, but I have to fly to Kuala Lumpur after the funeral."

"Was your uncle living in Kuala Lumpur?"

"Yes." Jeeva paused and then asked Neel hesitatingly. "You must have heard about his confinement."

At Neel's nod, Jeeva continued, "You know, uncle always insisted that he did not commit the crime and I was too young then to know the circumstance, but my mother trusted her brother. She told me that her brother would never do something like that."

"His sudden death must have shocked her."

"Yes, she is inconsolable."

'Your uncle…..Did he have any other relative?"

"No, he was single, and he stayed alone. He had an uncle, but he passed away some years ago."

"Don't you want to be with your mother during this family crisis?" Neel suggested

"She is the one who insisted that I be here to do the last rites. They were quite tight. My mother and her brother…And she believes that he was killed," Jeeva added thoughtfully.

Jeeva's words shocked Neel, "But didn't he suffer cardiac arrest?"

"Yeah that is what it looks like, but I have my doubts too. Let us wait for the report."

"What makes you think that it was not natural death?"

"My mother's family lived in Kuala Lumpur for many years. You can call them third or fourth generation Malaysian Indians. My mother married and moved to Fiji, but my uncle continued to live in Kuala Lumpur. He worked in their Police Force. There had been an excavation going on for constructing the present capital *Putrajaya*. The workers stumbled upon some ruins of a Hindu temple and some gold idols. My uncle, being a Tamilian, was entrusted with the job of bringing the treasures to Chennai because Tamil Nadu was demanding that Malaysia hand over the state assets. When he reached Chennai, a passenger travelling with him lost his baggage and my gullible uncle took him to his hotel. He stayed with him that night but in the morning, the man was dead, and the treasures were missing. My uncle was arrested for culpable homicide. He had served sentence for 24 years," Jeeva finished, visibly moved by his uncle's story and his tragic end.

Neel was quiet, giving Jeeva the space to overcome his emotions. When Jeeva took his leave, Neel assured him that he would attend the funeral.

****

Sindhoora reached home early that evening. Her parents were attending the wedding of a neighbour's son and she was to take care of her grandmother that evening. Adithya had his classes and she left her workplace as soon as the seminar concluded. Post dinner, she noticed that her grandmother was in deep thought and she was not concentrating on the soap-opera on the television,

"*Patti?*"

There was no response and she repeated, "*Patti…*"

Kalyani looked at her granddaughter and frowned, "Why are you shouting?"

Sindhoora grinned and held her grandmother in a tight hug, "Because you were lost in your own thoughts. And I called you many times, but you didn't respond." She explained still holding her grandmother and brushing her cheek against the older woman's head fondly.

Kalyani took Sindhoora's palms in her hands and replied affectionately, "I want to narrate an old story to my grandchildren, but they don't have time to listen to me, so I am wondering how to make them hear me out…"

"Awww….*Paati* I am always ready to listen to you. Why do you think I don't have time?"

"It is not just you Sindhu. I want both you and Adi with me when I narrate this old secret."

Sindhoora frowned at her. What was it that her grandmother

wanted to narrate? Was it about her uncle who cheated them? And her grandmother looked quite tense.

"What is it *Patti*? What is this secret you want to tell us?"

Her grandmother seemed lost in her own thoughts, while Sindhoora waited for her to speak. The doorbell rang, jolting them out of their contemplation. Assuming that it was her brother, Sindhoora opened the door. But it was Akhil.

"Who is it Sindhu? Is it Adithya?" her grandmother enquired loudly from her room, but Sindhu did not reply. Akhil barged inside and greeted her grandmother. Sindhoora followed him uncertainly. After small talk with her grandmother, he asked her to join him at the terrace.

On the terrace, Sindhoora had no idea what she was going to tell him, but some deep instinct warned her that it was not going to be pleasant.

"So, Sindhu, you were so busy that you had no time to talk to me?" his accusation did not call for a reply. He went on, "I confessed something very important to you and you did not even have the courtesy to reply to my messages or answer my calls. What kind of attitude are you showing me Sindhu?" Akhil asked her in frustration.

"What do you mean attitude Akhil? Your sudden confession threw me out of gear, and you expect me to give you a reply straight away?"

"I did not expect a reply, but you could have just told me that you needed time to think. Instead you started ignoring me. And I hate it when you ignore me Sindhu."

Sindhoora frowned at his words. "I was not ignoring you Akhil. I did not want to hurt you because I don't reciprocate the same feelings for you. I have never considered you more than my best friend."

While she was relieved that she had finally expressed her feelings, she had not anticipated his violent reaction.

He gripped her shoulders tightly and brought his face close to hers, "I love you Sindhu and I am sure that one day you will fall in love with me too."

"No Akhil I am not in love with you. What I feel for you is pure affection. And if you are going to mistake my friendship for something else, then it is not true," she tried to explain gently, while being careful not to hurt his feelings. But she did not succeed. He took her words to his heart and marched away in apparent rage and pain.

All alone in her room, she felt sad about the loss of their friendship. She doubted if they would ever regain their carefree days. A tear escaped her eyes at the memory of the scene on the terrace. She didn't know the reason, but she was very certain that she would never fall in love with Akhil. Before sleep claimed her, her mind valiantly fought the urge to learn about the well-being of Neel's mother.

****

Neel was determined to talk to his father, and he waited patiently for him to show up from work. Everyone else had retired for the night. His brother left town that morning to take part in a tennis match. Mahesh was an excellent tennis player and he won tournaments for the state. Neel checked on his mother and she was already fast asleep.

The house was quiet except for the rumble of air conditioners. His beloved brute 'Milo' was patrolling outside with his partner 'August'. Neel went back to the lounge and settled down with a magazine. His eyes fell on the family photograph and he picked up the photo frame. All the members of the family were assembled in the photo and it was clicked at the *Marina beach*. It was taken years ago when he was possibly 14 or 15 years old. His cousins were standing beside him in a row at the back. Standing next to him was Shreekant. Neel studied his cousin's face. He looked happy then but only a few days later he had taken his own life. The last note addressed to him by his cousin had haunted Neel for years. It still did. The concluding lines were imprinted on his mind.

"I hate you Nilu. I am leaving.

Having enslaved myself to you, I realize you have shown my place."

Suddenly Neel caught his breath. He tossed the magazine aside and raced to his room.

10) THE NIGHT OF CONTEMPLATION

"Emerging out of the lucent flame, like an omniscient you drove away that was wrong." Thirumurai 8 (1-1)

Rushing to his room, Neel extracted the note from the envelope.

"The slave, troubled in mind, roaming around the ancient forests

Cradling the alms-bowl, craved for the poison…"

A terrifying coldness clutched him in dread as the next lines of the verse fell into place…..

"Consumed by the fire with ignorance, descended down to the

End of the world, choking on struggling breath…."

It meant that he gasped for breath before succumbing to the overdose he had consumed. Everyone had figured that Shreekant took an overdose of the substance. Was it not affirmed by the doctors?

"The King of the tongue was saved by the holy bull,

Even if he did a lot of misdeeds due to ignorance,

But your boy could not be saved by the evil pull,

That destroyed him due to their emergence…."

The couplet tried to convey that Shreekant could not be saved from the evil force which Neel guessed was drug addiction. But who was this king of the tongue?

'That destroyed him due to their emergence'

What did it imply? Which force emerged and from where? Was it really about Shreekant or was Neel according too much importance to a note that was sent by someone at random?

He caught sight of the gold key that had arrived with this note. He examined it.

Neel recalled a vague memory of a similar key that he had found in Shreekant's room. Now as he recollected it, he rummaged for the old key in his room.

Where had he placed it? He looked back on that awful day when he had found his cousin dead. After searching his cousin's room, he had returned to his room, pocketing the key in his jeans. But he could not remember where he had placed the key after his grandfather left the room. He was ruminating about it when the knock on the door startled him.

It was his father, Chandra Shekhar, attired in a formal suit, he carried his laptop bag.

"Dad?"

"Yes, did you want to speak to me? Senthil informed me that you were waiting for me in the living room." Senthil was their manservant who had worked in the family for several years.

"Yeah dad, it is about mom."

Chandra Shekhar frowned and thrust the bag on the chair, "What about her?"

"Dad, do you know she has been getting chest pains and giddiness often for the past couple of months?"

"What?"

"Yes, we met the doctor yesterday. Her blood pressure was high, and she was asked to take things easy."

Chandra Shekhar was shocked. He was not aware that Revathi was going through stress and hypertension.

"What else did the doctor say?" he asked his eldest son in concern.

"Nothing more but she needs a break dad. She is shouldering too many responsibilities and she is managing everything alone. And dad, I think she is depressed."

"But Neel, there are several servants in the house to carry out the chores. Moreover, there is Saraswathi *athai* and Nalini to help her out. I don't understand why she is carrying the load on her shoulders single-handed."

"Dad, you are not listening to me. She is lonely and depressed. She needs something to occupy her time. And dad, you should have taken her to the U.S for a vacation."

"Oh, so she complained to you about me not taking her to visit you."

Neel sighed. This was so difficult. He wished his brother Mahesh was here. How do you make your parents understand your viewpoint without appearing partial?

"No, she did not complain about it. But she wanted to go on a holiday with you."

Chandra Shekhar slumped down on the chair and brushed his hair back. Neel noticed the lines of fatigue on his father's forehead.

"You don't understand Neel and neither does your mother. It is not easy to drop everything and go on a holiday. Every major decision of the business needs my approval and I can't forego my responsibilities. "

"Dad, there is your brother, brother-in-law and cousins. All of them are part of the organisation. So why don't you delegate your work?"

"Your grandfather wants me to keep tab on everything. I don't want to let him down on something that he and his ancestors have built so laboriously."

"Going on vacation will not cause any upheaval in the company. And these days everyone, right from Bill Gates to Zuckerberg, believes in short breaks with family. Or is it something else?"

Chandra Shekhar looked at his son warily, "What else could there be?"

"You tell me dad. You don't want to go on vacation. Do you? Why?" Chandra Shekhar regarded his son thoughtfully and paced the room restlessly.

"Dad… What is it?" Neel asked softly. There could be a number of reasons for his father's preoccupation with work, but Neel perceived that the emotional distance between his parents was hurting them both.

"Do you know that your mother blamed me for sending you abroad at such a young age?" Neel could see the hurt and pain in his father's eyes.

"Did she actually say so?"

"No, but I could feel it. Sometimes she missed you so much that she would cry at night. But when I tried to talk to her, she would reject my overtures. What could I do Neel? I could not have gone against my father's decision. She didn't realise that I too missed you."

"Dad, I don't think mom blamed you. She understood your predicament."

"Did she say so?" Chandra Shekhar asked his son eagerly.

"No but you need to talk to her. She is bottling up too many things and that is not good for her health."

"Your presence here will bring a refreshing transition. It will make a difference to your mother definitely. Shreekant's death left a huge void in this family. Things have never been the same since then."

Neel was in a quandary about whether he should confide his plans to his father, "Dad, which is what I was going to talk to you about. I will have to return to U.S. The company requires my presence there."

There was only silence in the room. His father considered him quietly and asked, "So why bother about your mother or me? You are leaving anyway."

"Dad, you know it is not like that."

"No Neel, you have gone way too far from us now. You don't feel comfortable here anymore. And I don't blame you. We can't expect you to drop everything and come back now that we need you."

"Of course, I am here if you need me, but I just can't work here."

"Neel, I am not pressurizing you emotionally, but the business here does need fresh blood. I am proud of the way you have built up an organisation successfully in a foreign country without any guidance or help from the family. It's not just me; your grandfather is also extremely proud of you. There is not a single person to whom he has not extolled your virtues."

"Thanks dad…."

"And Neel we need someone dynamic like you to handle the present crisis."

The word 'crisis' seized his attention, "What crisis?"

"We are losing money! There has been embezzlement in the company, and we have not yet found the culprit. Several of our enterprises are running at loss. Every time we aim to clinch a government contract, the deal slips away from our hands. Someone inside our organisations is playing dirty. And we have invested in too many projects indiscriminately. I can feel the company sliding from our grip and I don't know how I will face your grandfather."

Neel was aghast at the hopelessness he saw in his father's eyes. Earlier, he had been concerned about his mother's health, but now he was more worried about his father's despondency.

"Dad, it can't be so bad. There must be ways to salvage it."

"I don't even know whom to trust to discuss about it."

"What do you mean? The family is on the board of the company so it could be a united effort from all family members," Neel suggested hopefully. He had been under the impression that *'Thillai Group of Industries'* was a flourishing organisation but to his dismay the company was underperforming.

His father laughed and for the first time Neel noticed the disillusionment and cynicism in his father's eyes. Neel had always considered his father a winner in life, but he seemed broken now.

"How naïve you are Neel! Money and power can change all equations."

Chandra Shekhar picked up his bag as Neel tried to comprehend his father's bitter words. Neel halted him, "Dad, do you want me to work here?"

"No Neel, I would never ask you to give up on your dream. But yes, you are someone I would have trusted immensely. Don't fret over what I said. Think of it as an ageing guy's rant." His father tried to make light of his worries, but Neel saw through his valiant effort.

"Dad, you are not that old."

Chandra Shekhar smiled at his son warmly and patted his back, "Don't worry about mom. I will talk to her."

Neel could not forget his father's bleak words that betrayed his bitterness. Neel went for a long drive that night. He parked the car near *Eliot's beach* and sat on a stone culvert, gazing at the distant moon and the sea. He realised that he would never be at peace with himself if he left the country and his parents in the present state. He was not certain if his presence would help them, but his conscience did not allow him to desert them when they needed him the most. May be he was assuming too much self-importance, but he could not dismiss his father's anguish or his mother's forlornness. His father mentioned that money and power could change all equations. Did he mean that someone in the family was playing foul? And why did he not discuss everything candidly with his grandfather?

He felt the tangy whisper of breeze on his face. He was the only one present on the beach and it was that hour of the night when every soul on the earth rested their consciousness momentarily. Even the ocean seemed to have gone on a slumber. There was a lull in the lashing waves and the sailing clouds covered the moon partly. The church bell tolled softly in the mild gust of the wind and the tranquility of the moment gripped Neel with an unknown surge of energy. The stillness of the hour, the call of the duty and the wrench of emotions encompassed him with their profoundness. He didn't know how long he remained in contemplation.

But he made the most important decision of his life.

Yes, he would stay back. He would ask his partners in the U.S.A to manage his company on his behalf for some months.

From somewhere a bird chirped its first wake up call. The night had come to its end and dawn was on its way. Neel walked toward the ocean and bent down to touch the cold water, splashing his hands and feet with it. He felt pleased with his decision.

****

Sindhoora woke up late that morning. She had been tossing and turning over Akhil's demeanour. He had refused to accept her lack of interest in him and that worried her. She kept fretting about it and as a result she overslept that morning. She rushed for work at a frenetic pace. The upcoming *Pongal* holidays spurred her to complete the assignments that day. When she reached office, she was asked to substitute for the receptionist who was on leave, for a couple of hours.

Sindhoora never realised that a receptionist's job was so difficult. She did not get a moment's respite that morning. At the end of the two hours, another girl arrived to assume charge. While Sindhoora explained the details in the logbook, the phone shrieked and she grabbed it,

"Good morning, *The Bay's Architects*," Sindhoora answered automatically while handing over the charges to the other girl.

"Can I speak to Mr. Balachander?" The caller asked and his deep voice sounded familiar to Sindhoora.

"He is not in office at the moment. Can I connect you to someone else please?" Sindhoora wondered where she had heard his voice.

"Who am I speaking to?"

"Sindhoora Vaidyanathan"

There was silence at the other end, and she frowned at the phone.

"Shall I take down a message?" She asked

"Yes, this is Neel Chandra from *Thillai Group of Industries*. Ask Balachander to call me." And the line was disconnected.

She stared at the phone. Neel Chandra? Was he the one with the long mane of hair? And the sound of his voice!

****

Neel flung his cell phone on the bed and wondered if all the girls in the city were named Sindhoora. Was she working in '*The Bay's Architects*'? He hoped that it was not the same bothersome girl.

In vexation, he strode to his grandfather's room. Arunachalam was astonished to see his grandson in a dark formal suit with trimmed hair and clean-shaven face.

****

In the dense forest, a lone man dropped a couple of lighted cigarette butts on the dried grass and hurried back to the plains, making sure to not cross paths with anyone. There were dried leaves near the pit, and he was sure that the cigarettes he dropped would spark a fire. The humidity was low and the high -speed wind was perfect for the spark he had left to become highly inflammable.

He rode the bicycle fast on the isolated stretch of road and breathed a sigh of relief when he reached the bus stand at the nearest village. While he ordered a cup of tea, he noticed the group of trekkers alighting from the bus and heading towards the range of forest he had just left behind.

11) SUICIDE OR MURDER

"With the universe chanting his name, he is the glittering start of life everlasting!" Thirumurai 8 (1-1)

"Nilagriva, you look so handsome!" Neel's grandfather exclaimed.

"My stint in 'Thillai Industries' begins today."

"Ah finally! So, have you come to seek my blessings Nilagriva?"

"Maybe! And please stop calling me Nilagriva. It is Neel now."

"No, I won't. You may be *Neel* to others but for me you will always be that *Nilagriva* for whom your grandmother and I prayed. No one can alter it. Not even you." Arunachalam stressed remembering the days before Nilagriva's birth when he and his wife had visited every temple of Lord Neelakanta for a healthy child.

Neel sighed. His grandfather was an obstinate man. "I will not respond if you keep up with your stubbornness."

His grandfather laughed aloud, "We will see Nilagriva…." The challenge excited Arunachalam.

Neel regarded his grandfather with dry amusement. His grandfather was a law unto himself. He empathized with his father for hesitating to discuss business with him.

"That American girl who came with you, has she left?" Arunachalam asked and Neel's eyes flared with displeasure, "Her name is Ann and yes she has left. Why?"

"Are you in love with her?"

"With who?"

"That American girl?" Seeing the exasperation on his grandson's face he corrected himself, "Ok Ok Ann."

"No, I am not. And what if I was?"

"But you are not, and I am happy. She is no good for you."

Neel walked out of the room before he lost his temper. His grandfather could be malicious sometimes. Many of his relatives feared him. Arunachalam could tear one to pieces with his outrageous and scornful words.

When Neel announced his intentions to his parents that morning, he did not expect that his decision would elicit such a heart-warming response from them. His father looked as if somebody had injected a new dose of vigour into him.

Revathi was ecstatic about Neel's decision. When Neel left for higher studies, all of them had drifted away from each other. Mahesh had missed the presence of his elder brother whom he had hero-worshipped for so long. Chandra Shekhar and Revathi had missed the supporting shoulder of their son; their pride and their strength as the years passed.

****

Arunachalam was reading the newspaper when his eldest daughter marched into the room. She seemed furious and disturbed. Arunachalam sighed and folded the paper. Saraswathy always had a bone to pick with someone in the house. It would be either one of the servants or one of his daughters-in-law, Nalini or Revathi.

"Appa, how can you allow Neel to work for the company?"

Arunachalam frowned at his eldest daughter, "Why not Saraswathy?

It is his right and prerogative to join our business." Arunachalam could not understand the reason behind his daughter's fury. Since Neel returned from the U.S, he had noticed his daughter growing increasingly distraught.

"No *appa,* I will not allow Neel to work here. He is living Shreekant's life."

Arunachalam caught his breath at his daughter's words. His eyes scanned her face and there was bitterness and grief writ large on it. She had never recovered from the brutal blow that life had dealt her. And he could feel her pain. He wished that there was something he could do to ease her pain. He glanced at his wife's portrait hoping to find some answer in the eyes that stared back at him.

"Saraswathy, I understand your pain. Shreekant was my grandson as well and I have gone through the same agony. But that does not mean that Neel can't lead his own life dear."

"You don't understand *Appa.*"

"What is it that I don't understand dear?" Arunachalam was taken aback when Saraswathy started weeping. Her shoulders sagged and she buried her face in the *pallu* of her cotton *sari.*

"Oh no dear…" Arunachalam comforted his daughter and guided her toward the couch. He offered her a glass of water and asked her to calm down.

"What is it Saraswathy? Tell me. What is bothering you?"

"*Appa,* I can't tell you. You won't be able to accept it."

"Don't you know your father dear? I am as strong as the mangroves of *Pichavaram.* No Tsunami can disturb me. Tell me."

Saraswathy's wan smile at her father's attempt to cheer her did not go unnoticed by Arunachalam. He waited patiently for her to speak,

"Appa, it was Neel who killed my son Shreekant."

****

Neel paused and looked out of the window as the car halted at the traffic signal. He was travelling with his father to his office and it being his first day, his father explained the infrastructure of the company they were visiting this morning. But when Neel looked at the traffic signal, it was not work or office that crossed his thoughts. He regarded the spot and checked to see if it was the same traffic cop. He didn't remember the face of the traffic constable, but he recollected every feature of the face that fixed him with furious doe eyes. He sighed wistfully. It was the same junction where he had saved her from approaching cars. She had dismissed him when he had asked if she was a social worker. She had again dismissed him at the temple when they exchanged heated words. It was written all over that Sindhoora did not like Neel Chandra. Maybe that was what interested him about her. He had never faced a girl who looked at him as though he was an annoying punk. He combed his fingers through his hair. She had not even had the courtesy to thank him, but then he had not thanked her either, for taking care of his mother in the auditorium. And she did look after his mother well. No two ways about it, he had to admit to himself. His mother still mentioned her at times.

His father observed the amused look on his son's face and asked, "Neel what are you amused about?"

"Nothing dad... Somebody called me a punk once."

"Well, you are one," his father stated in good humour.

"Dad!"

And after a long time, Neel saw his father laughing whole-heartedly.

****

"What nonsense are you saying Saraswathy? Have you gone crazy?" Arunachalam asked his daughter in shock.

He closed the door of his room swiftly.

"See I told you that you will not believe it."

"Of course, I will not believe it. Do you even know what you are uttering? Think before you speak such rubbish."

"*Appa* I have proof that it was Neel who did it."

Arunachalam could not believe that his daughter was pointing an accusing finger at his Nilagriva. The boy whose birth had granted such joy to him and his wife!

"What proof?" he asked in bewilderment. That horrible day when he had found his other grandson Shreekant lifeless was etched on his mind.

Saraswathy rushed to her room. She was back ten minutes later.

"See this. I found this in Neel's jeans pockets that day."

Arunachalam looked at her outstretched palm which held a key. He frowned and picked it up. Shaped like a flag staff, the gold key had a tiny bull welded in a sitting posture at one end. It looked more like a souvenir than a functional key. It had a loop at one end which pointed to the fact that it was used as a locket.

"Saraswathy, how does this key prove that it was Nilagriva who had a hand in Shreekant's death? The doctors acknowledged that it was an overdose of that drug that Shreekant had consumed."

"I know what the doctors said, but I saw Neel searching for it in Shreekant's room that night. I wondered what it was that he was looking for so desperately. Then next day, I found this in his jeans' pocket."

Arunachalam studied the key thoughtfully, coming to a conclusion. "Let me talk to Neel. Then we will know."

Saraswathy smiled with skepticism, "And you think he is going to acknowledge it?"

Arunachalam frowned at his daughter, "Why do you hate him so much? He is your nephew Saraswathy."

Saraswathy glared at her father with all the hatred buried deep inside her heart, "Because he does not have the right to live when my son is dead."

With those damning words, she rushed out of the room. Arunachalam froze in crushing silence as his daughter's words slowly sunk into him.

****

Since her visit to the hospital, Kalyani had been in a dilemma. She pondered if it was time to reveal the cabalistic significance to her grandchildren! How long was she going to live? What if one day she closed her eyes forever without divulging the esoteric knowledge that she possessed to her grand-children? Her father would never forgive her, and neither would his father. It was a tradition to pass it on to the next generation. She could have entrusted it with her son Vaidya. But she didn't want to appear partial or biased. Her younger son who had abandoned her and who had cheated his siblings out of the property did not deserve to be entrusted with something so sacred and venerated for years through generations. And if she divulged it to Vaidya alone, then her daughter would be hurt. She didn't think Adithya would believe it. Her eldest granddaughter (Sindhoora's sister) was living in another city, so it was out of question. Her daughter's sons Akhil and Ganesh were not the ones to be trusted with something so hallowed. So, she decided to divulge the truth to Sindhoora.

****

Neel attended the funeral service of Arumugam. Other than the priest and a police officer, he and Jeeva were the only ones present there. After the ceremony, Jeeva thanked him for his gesture. While they talked about Arumugam, the police officer handed over an envelope which contained the detailed report of the post-mortem.

Jeeva was shocked at the analysis and asked Neel to read it. Neel read it with growing skepticism and dismay. He looked at Jeeva's disturbed face and asked, "Does this mean overdose?"

"Yes, and he was not into drugs," Jeeva affirmed emotionally.

Neel read the report once again; the report showed traces of mercury along with an overdose of drug called Xanax.

"Mercury? And what is Xanax?"

"It is a Benzodiazepine drug, meaning a tranquilizer or anti-depressant."

The police officer joined them and instructed Jeeva to meet him at the police station for the details and routine procedure.

"The officer is insisting that it is a case of suicide and that they are planning to shut the file on him. They are saying that my uncle might have obtained the drug in the prison," Jeeva explained as they walked back to the car.

"What is the doctor saying?" Neel asked.

"The doctor says that if it was just a case of drugs overdose, then it could be suicide. But he is suspicious about my uncle obtaining Mercury. I don't understand why anyone would take mercury?"

"So, just as you suspected, it could be murder."

"Yes, and I am sure that it was murder by conspiracy," said Jeeva emphatically as they drove to the police station.

****

Udayarajan glared at the manager with impatience. He reflected over the reason for employing such idiots in his office. His firm *The Bay's Architect* was one of the biggest landscape firms in Chennai. So, there was no question of anyone denying him access to any part of that area.

"I can't believe that the administration denied your request. How the hell did you approach them?"

"Sir, we followed every protocol and the company's authorisation letter was sent to them. Still they refused."

"Give me the number. Let me talk to them. I want to develop the area into a resort. I know the architects have the blueprint for the area. But I want to buy this land from the owners. These mangroves can be razed, and a beautiful lake can be carved in the spot."

"Sir, it is illegal to destroy the mangroves."

"Who says so? The State? Give me some credit Balachander."

The man scratched his head as he produced the plan for the resort. After he left, Udayarajan studied the plan on the blueprint. What did Balachander think about him? That he was an ignorant fool? Didn't Balachander know that Udayarajan was an expert at the rules and regulations of the land?

He looked at the name of the owner of the estate. With a malicious grin, he read it aloud,

'*Arunachalam Chidambaram Chettiar*'

He was killing two birds with one stone. After extensive search of old records, Udayarajan and his brother focused on their mission to destroy Arunachalam and his family. They had been searching for the family for many years and when they were certain that it was Arunachalam that they had looked for, they had set about to destroy him. Some of the businesses of the industrialist were running at a loss because Udayarajan had planted a mole in their organization. He was leaking information about their business to Udayarajan and he had systematically managed to thwart the attempts of *Thillai Group* to procure Government tenders. But Arunachalam's misfortunes had begun with the death of his grandson many years ago.

It was the beginning of the end.

12) SINDHOORA VAIDYANATHAN

"Bound to you by my devotion, bliss and sorrow – the travails of life cannot shake me." Thirumurai 5 (1-4)

After the formalities at the police station were completed, Jeeva considered his next course of action. Although he was disturbed about the results of the autopsy report, he could not take any action immediately. He had to board a flight in the evening for Kuala Lumpur.

"I don't know what to do now. The police have shut the file, concluding it to be suicide, but I reckon it is murder. Two days before my uncle died, I had asked him to go with me to Fiji, but he refused. He said he had unfinished business here and that he would complete his work before visiting my mother in Fiji. I am breaking my head over what could have happened to him in those two days?" Jeeva shared his thoughts with Neel.

"He could have confronted the people who had put him behind bars, and they might have had a hand in his death. It is one probable theory that I can come up with. And the overdose report? How did they do it?" Neel wondered aloud, as thoughts of his cousin's death from the past troubled him.

"That is what is confusing me. Did they inject him with it? Was he not aware of it?"

Neel drove in silence comparing Arumugam's and Shreekant's deaths. Did someone else induce Shreekant's overdose? What about the cryptic message that he received from an unknown sender?

Taking a break from conflicting thoughts about his cousin, Neel asked Jeeva, "What are your plans for the day? Do you want me to drop you somewhere?"

Jeeva shrugged, "I don't know. My flight is at 9pm and I have checked out of my room. I will have to collect my luggage from the reception and head to airport. You can drop me at the hotel now. I will spend the day in their lounge."

But Neel was hesitant to let Jeeva wander alone in the city after his uncle Arumugam's death. He remembered Arumugam's friendly overtures at the pub. He had not looked as if he was going to kill himself. A wish to ease Jeeva's troubles motivated Neel to offer his help.

"Why don't you keep me company till the evening and I will drop you at the airport?" Neel offered

Jeeva regarded Neel's face and asked, "Why do you want to be stuck with me? I mean don't you have other things to do?"

"You can accompany me to work. I don't mind if you are ok with it."

Jeeva did not mind. In fact, he liked Neel Chandra. There was something very candid and forthright about him. He accepted Neel's offer.

"Tell me one thing Neel. Your accent is so American. You are not from this part of the world?"

Neel was amused, "I belong to this part, but I spent many years in the U.S."

"Ah! No wonder! Sorry if I got too personal. Initially I thought you were trying to impress one and all."

"You really thought I was trying to impress?" And Neel wondered if everyone he met since his arrival from the U.S thought he was showing off.

Jeeva was embarrassed and apologized, "Sorry my bad….What happened to your Jared Leto hair style?"

"Chopped them off! If I appeared like that in offices, I would be barred from meeting anyone here." Jeeva laughed at Neel's joke and a quick camaraderie developed between the two young men.

Neel drove to the office where he had an appointment with Balachander. He had been studying the financial position of companies that the family owned and narrowed down to three companies, which were running at huge losses. The first company was the one developing their properties into luxury resorts and hotels. Neel had discussions with the board and the chief executive officer of the company, learning details of the firm called *'The Bay's Architects'* outsourced by them for landscaping and outdoor designing. There was a property on the outskirts of Chennai that the firm was landscaping for a resort.

He was meeting their officer that afternoon. He parked the car and checked his face and hair.

"Are you coming?" he asked Jeeva.

"Yes, it looks swanky and I won't mind some air-conditioning. It is hot here man."

As they stepped into the cool interiors, Neel realised that he had been tense and holding his breath in anticipation. To his chagrin, his eyes, of their own will, searched for a slim, striking girl whose doe eyes and heart-shaped face had invaded his thoughts many a time. He sighed with relief at the sight of another girl on the desk. The girl led him to the cabin of Balachander.

****

Jeeva relaxed on the settee in the lounge and skimmed through the glossy pages of a magazine that was lying on the coffee table. His mind was on his journey to Kuala Lumpur. His first assignment would be to search his uncle's house for some incriminating evidence. Then he would talk to his uncle's colleagues who had worked with him twenty-five years ago. The telephone ring on the reception desk jolted him out of his thoughts and he regarded the receptionist who smiled at him coyly. She offered him a cup of tea and he accepted it gladly. He was aware that he made an arresting picture with his jeans, T-shirt and tattooed arms. His light eyes made him stand out and like always he enjoyed the girl's attention.

The receptionist dialed a number and rattled away in urgency to the other person. Jeeva was transported to his life in Fiji. Life in Fiji was not so frenzied and the pace in his country was generally relaxed and laid back. He supposed that it depended on the priorities one had in life. While he mulled about the contrasting lives in the two countries, he noticed a girl rushing in with files and documents. She did not see him and leaned on the reception counter to talk to the receptionist. What attracted Jeeva to her was her thick lustrous black hair. They were left open and glistened with vitality. The girl at the reception whispered something in her ear and she turned back to look at him. Jeeva caught his breath as he felt the sudden rush of adrenaline in his blood. He stared unabashedly at her and it was the first time in his life that he was so captivated by a girl. Her dark eyes, small face and pointed chin bewitched him. The slender figure in trendy Indian wear heightened her allure.

****

Sindhoora was embarrassed. The man stared at her as if he had not seen a woman before. Her irritated glare did not deter him from admiring her. She turned back, collected the copies from the receptionist and headed to Balachander's office ignoring the stranger. She had learnt that *'Thillai group of companies'* was an important client to her firm and no one took them lightly. She checked her attire in the mirror of the elevator. It was not every day that one gets to visit the big boss in his office. Her pastel blue leggings and the princess line, long *kurta* in tangerine blue enhanced her slim figure. Her hair was wet, so she had left it open in the morning after the shampoo wash. Her *kohl* lined eyes stared out of her heart-shaped face. She wrinkled her nose and brushed her hair back. The elevator came to a stop and she headed to Balachander's office. She knocked on the door before opening it tentatively. She entered with the files hardly noticing the formally attired man on the chair opposite her boss. She registered the broad shoulder and grey blazer vaguely. Her attention was on her boss who waited impatiently for the documents. She handed him the documents and stood beside the huge glass-topped table with files and documents, searching for the sheets her boss asked for.

"Sit down Sindhoora and give me the details of measurements you collected on your field visit."

Sindhoora pulled the chair and sat down still not noticing the client. She studied the documents while her boss addressed his visitor.

"So, Neel these are the details…"

Sindhoora's face shot up at the name and noticed the suited man properly. Her jaw dropped as she gaped at him. He looked so different. His long mane of hair was trimmed, and his short hair was brushed back neatly. Instead of the usual jeans, he was dressed in a formal suit. What was he doing here? She asked herself.

****

If Neel Chandra had to capture a moment and freeze it, he would have done it at the spot precisely. Her expression was a sight to behold. He made an effort to control his mirth at her shock and consequent recognition. It was absolutely comical, though there was nothing comical about her. From the moment she entered the room, he was transfixed by her enrapturing appearance: the open hair and dark eyes had made it impossible to look away from her face. Thankfully she did not notice his interest. She had been too busy providing details to Balachander. He sighed. Did he really envy the man for having her work for him? He did not think so.

Now as they stared at each other, he gave her a dry, amused half-smile. Her eyes widened at his smile and she narrowed her eyes thoughtfully.

"Sindhoora read out the details of the project," her boss demanded.

"Sir, this property covers almost five acres of land and the adjoining lake borders the property at the south-east end. The villagers have agreed to move out of their dwellings for the price that we quoted and according to our agreement, water would be freely available if they need it. The rare breed of Grey Pelicans that we identified in the area would be provided with an alternative resting place."

Neel listened to her quietly while Balachander raved about the advantages of landscaping the property.

"Mr. Balachander, I don't want to develop the property into any resort. Let us cancel the contract. We plan to re-sell the land to its original owners."

Neel's request shocked Balachander. "But Neel, we have already done the landscaping and we have almost completed the planting of saplings."

"I know and I am sorry for the wasted efforts, but we can't go ahead with this project. We will be pulling out of it and putting up the property for sale soon."

"But you can't do this……"

"Can't do this?" Neel asked him coldly, "What do you mean?" He stood up; all the time aware of Sindhoora listening to their conversation.

"I will have to speak to my Chairman. Mr. Udayarajan will be furious."

"Fix an appointment with him and I will discuss with him," Neel concluded as he shook hands with Balachander and strode out of the room. Sindhoora followed him as Balachander asked her to close the door on her way out. Sindhoora guessed that he wanted to speak to his boss alone.

She saw Neel waiting for the lift and walked up to him. He glanced at her and she blurted out, "It is good that you are not developing the property into a resort."

Neel waited for further explanation as the lift door opened. They stepped in and Sindhoora continued, "It is a haven for migratory birds and a breeding ground for them. Some ten rare species of birds visit the place every year. Have you visited the place during winter? It is a pleasure to see so many of them fluttering around and chirping joyously. I love the place."

Neel was listening half-heartedly because his attention was riveted by her animated eyes and excited chatter.

"Why didn't you say this in front of your boss?" Neel interrupted her flow of excitement with his matter of fact question. She paused and realised who she was talking to, "We don't get paid to talk about migratory birds and their habits." Her retort egged him to ask, "So you love the place?"

The lift stopped, "Yes I love it, but I would hate for it to be developed into a resort because the villagers would lose their direct access to water and their land would be snatched away from them," she replied softly.

Neel turned to her, his eyes glinting at her icily "Are you a socialist? They are getting paid for their piece of land and they have agreed to let go of their access to water through that strip of land."

"Yes, I know it is a rich man's world," she took a jibe at him in return and marched ahead without waiting for his reaction. Neel gritted his teeth at her provoking words and strode forward to meet Jeeva at the lobby.

"Sorry that took so long," he apologized but he noticed that Jeeva had become quite friendly with the receptionist and was chatting to her.

They exited the building and Jeeva grinned at him, "Guess what?"

"What?" Neel asked placing the laptop on the back seat of the car.

"I met my dream girl and I am coming back here to meet her definitely."

"Really? That is an achievement for the day, and I am glad that I could be of help in finding her for you," Neel replied drily, amused at Jeeva's excitement.

"Yes." Jeeva climbed on the front seat and as soon as he took the seat, he yelped, *"Ouch!"* He jumped out of the car and peered at the seat. Neel scowled wondering what the matter was...

Jeeva picked up something and studied it, "How the hell did this come here?" He was about to throw it away when Neel shouted, "Wait…"

Neel came around the car and snatched it from Jeeva. It was a small needle. Neel was shocked. He placed the needle carefully at the top of the dash-board and asked Jeeva urgently, "Jeeva, did it prick you?" When Jeeva nodded, Neel pulled him back to the lobby of the office and asked the receptionist to call an ambulance immediately. The girl fumbled and he asked her to call Sindhoora Vaidyanathan.

When he caught sight of Sindhoora, he demanded her to call an ambulance urgently, "It is urgent Sindhoora. He has been injected with poison." He pointed at his friend, "And please, give us some tissues." When Sindhoora handed him the paper napkins he urged her to talk to his friend. "Keep talking to him. I will be back in a minute."

Sindhoora looked at his friend and recognized him as the man who had stared at her candidly earlier. He looked pale now and Sindhoora asked him to take a seat. He slumped down, but she did not allow him to close his eyes. The receptionist also joined her, and they kept talking to him though he didn't appear to be listening.

Neel raced to his car, placed the needle carefully in the napkins and wrapped it. The ambulance arrived and the paramedics took care of Jeeva. By the time they reached hospital, Jeeva was almost unconscious.

13) THE ENCHANTING MOON

"*Like the graceful swans that are washed with the pearly fluorescence of the moon, amidst the soaring towers of the city.*" *Thirumurai 11 (1-1)*

That night when Sindhoora gazed at the star-studded sky, she wondered if Neel was able to save his friend. She hoped that he was successful.

There was something intoxicating about the silvery bright night. From somewhere she heard a song playing in the FM and she listened to its lyrics.

Even though the beautiful moon is visible,

There is no one but me enjoying the vision,

Even though the night is breezy, and the stars are smiling,

There is no one but me who is appreciating it...

The melodious song could be heard from the room across the terrace. Sindhoora loved good music and she did not mind if it was in Hindi, English or Tamil.

The lyrics seemed to echo her appreciation of the night. She recounted her meeting with Neel in the office and wished that she had been smarter and wittier. She climbed down to her tiny room in the first floor of the house. The room had a narrow balcony with wooden railings. She did not open the door of the balcony often because it would expose her room directly to the road. Her small room was decorated with strings of lights and hanging pots of plants. The mattress on the floor occupied one length of the wall and it was strewn with a number of small cushions made by her.

Except for a vintage teak wood *almirah,* the room was bare of any other furniture. The sloping wooden ceiling, which was common in old structures, retained the coolness inside the room. The winding wooden stairs from the ground floor *veranda* branched into two rooms on the first-floor landing. One was her room and the other was her parents' room. Adithya and her grandmother used the rooms on the ground floor. The rows of houses with common walls like these were standard in most of the streets surrounding temples in the villages and cities of Tamil Nadu. They were called *Agraharams*, and the houses were built on land donated by noble men or kings to families, particularly Brahmins who performed religious duties in temples. Times changed and so did their professions, but families like hers continued to live in such localities.

Like her father, many families had altered the houses with modern structures that included grilled enclosure in the *veranda* and concrete roofing of the ceiling. Her room was the only one in the house with wooden ceiling. Her grandmother called her room *'Macchil Kucchil'* teasingly, meaning an attic. When Sindhoora got her periods, her grandmother banished her to this attic and banned her from entering the kitchen, an old custom still practiced among many families. Sindhoora did not believe in following such archaic customs, so she had stopped informing her grandmother about her periods over the last couple of years.

Now as she settled on her comfortable floor bed, she opened her laptop and searched for *'Thillai Group of Companies'*. Many pages opened up and there were plenty of news items on the group, about their business acquisitions and new ventures. She peered at the screen as she enlarged the pictures and scanned the information about the founder of the company. Arunachalam Chidambaram Chettiar looked tall and regal in the picture and as she learnt the details of his family, she frowned. There was no one called Neel

Chandra in the family. Arunachalam Chettiar had two sons, two daughters and five grandchildren. His grandchildren were Nilagriva Chandra Shekhar, Maheshwara Chandra Shekhar, Kalpana Shanmugam, Geeta Subramaniam and Kartik Subramaniam. So, if Neel was not family, did he work for the company? She pondered browsing for the name Neel Chandra on different websites. There were a few pages that opened up, but they were not the Neel Chandra she was looking for. She guessed that he had locked his social media accounts. Her mobile ring disturbed her from her exploration, and she answered the call without noticing the unknown number.

"Hello"

"Hi" She didn't recognize the voice but noted the unknown number and answered hesitatingly, "Hi"

"Neel Chandra here… I wanted to thank you for helping my friend today."

Sindhoora was thrown off-balance by his call and she was tongue-tied momentarily.

"Hello!" Neel repeated and she somehow recovered her lost voice.

"Hi, how is your friend?"

"Better. They have flushed out the poison. He is under observation tonight."

"Oh…" She could not come up with anything else.

"Did I disturb you from your sleep?" Neel asked and she cursed herself silently for being such a dimwit.

"No no, I was working. So how was he poisoned?" She asked as common sense asserted itself over her flummoxed brain.

"He was injected."

"And your mother? How is she?" Sindhoora asked as the events of the other evening touched her memory.

"She is taking medicines for hyper-tension."

"Is that why she fainted?"

"Yes." There was a pause and then he continued, "Anyway, thanks for helping me Sindhoora. Goodnight" And the call was disconnected. She glared at her smart phone, wondering why he disconnected the call so abruptly. Did she say something wrong? Well, she supposed he did not like her talking about his mother's health. But how did he get her number? She saved his number in her contact list.

Her last thought before sleep claimed her was that next time she would try to be more engaging, rather than sound dumb and stupid.

****

Jeeva Velu Stane was fortunate enough to be taken to the hospital promptly and have the poison flushed out of his body. Neel had handed over the needle to the doctor and they had asked him to wait for a couple of days for the results.

Neel requested Jeeva to postpone his journey to Kuala Lumpur but Jeeva was not willing to delay his inquest into his uncle's death. He was convinced now that his uncle was murdered. Someone was attempting to kill Jeeva now.

"No Neel, I need to take this journey immediately because I want to catch the rascals as soon as possible. I am certain that they are after my blood now. I feel there was something in uncle's possession that they wanted badly."

"I cancelled your seat in last night's flight. When do you want to go now?" Neel asked Jeeva as they waited for the discharge formalities to be completed at the hospital next morning.

"Maybe tonight! I have to go to the hotel to collect my luggage. And Neel thanks for taking care of me. I would not be alive if it had not been for your prompt action." Jeeva was grateful that Neel had recognized that poisonous needle and taken him to hospital immediately. Even now, he felt disoriented after the treatment at the hospital.

"You know it is really strange. I mean the similarity between your uncle's collapse and your condition last afternoon!"

Jeeva frowned and looked at Neel curiously, "Meaning?"

"Both the times, I was in the vicinity."

Neel insisted on paying the bill and they exited the hospital two hours later. Jeeva checked the seat before moving into the car. It was a different car and when Jeeva asked him about it, Neel explained, "I have given the other car to the workshop. I asked them to change the upholstery. I didn't want to take any chance."

"True, it is better to be cautious. So, what were you saying? What if you were in the vicinity? I don't get your point."

"Someone could be trying to frame me for the attacks."

Neel was reminded of the note of his cousin where he had blamed him for his plight.

"What? But why would anyone do that Neel?"

"Don't know. I am baffled by the way the needle found its way into my car."

They collected Jeeva's luggage and headed to the airport. Jeeva managed to get a seat in the flight that was leaving late evening to Kuala Lumpur via Colombo. Jeeva thanked Neel once again before departing into the lounge.

"Thanks man for all the help. I hope we will meet sometime soon."

"Sure, we will. Don't you want to meet your dream girl? You said you were coming back," Neel teased him.

"Oh yes but I don't remember anything much after the needle episode. So, let us hope that she will come to Fiji," Jeeva sighed remembering the enchanting face of the girl vaguely.

"Take care Jeeva."

****

After dropping Jeeva at the airport, Neel headed home to discuss his meetings with his father. Ann had called him the previous night to express her pleasure while visiting places like Jaipur and Jodhpur. She was thrilled to bits about her trip. She had also wanted to know if he missed her. Neel sighed as he drove on the highway. The traffic was at its peak and he switched on his stereo. Although he had replied that he had been too busy, a voice in his head chided him for lying to her. He had not been too busy to think about Sindhoora. He ran his fingers through his hair and stared at the small crowd that was crossing the road. Why was he so drawn to Sindhoora? Last night, over the phone she had sounded too distant, so he had disconnected the call.

One of his old favourite songs filled the car with their lyrical and breezy notes,

Your eyes speak million things to me,

As I long for your love;

Under the moon-lit sky and dancing stars,

I want to confess my love

To make you mine forever…

Her dark eyes spoke their own language, sometimes furious, like how they were at the temple, sometimes compassionate like when she had been with his mother, and sometimes animated, like when she was at her office. They glittered like a mid-summer night star and stirred him with their appeal. Such feelings for her disrupted his composure. He jammed his feet on the brakes as he entered the fort like gates of his house. He was angry for allowing such thoughts to assail him.

When he entered the drawing-room, he saw Shubashri chatting with his brother and uncle. "Ah Neel, there you are. *Thatha* is searching for you." Mahesh called out to him. "And Neel we are going for a movie tonight. We are booking ticket for you too."

"Nope, I am not coming. I have some work to finish," he replied pondering the reason behind his grandfather wanting to meet him.

"Neel, it will be fun. Do come with us. We haven't spent time with you lately," Shubashri's request surprised him. She never spoke much, especially when he was around.

Neel smiled at her politely and replied, "Sorry, I have a lot of things to complete. Perhaps another time!"

His aunt Saraswathy, whom he had not noticed, spoke from the doorway, "Neel you can't be so busy. Devote some time to Shubashri also. She has been looking forward to this outing."

Neel regarded his aunt with surprise. It was the first time that she was speaking at length to him after his arrival. Shubashri looked at him coyly with a teasing smile. Neel frowned as Mahesh glanced at him playfully. He speculated about their glances and smiles. Looking at his aunt he replied, "I am sorry, but there is a meeting tomorrow, so I have to work on it." He gave a regretful nod to Shubashri.

****

Sindhoora's head was filled with thoughts of Neel Chandra. She was not able to concentrate on her work. She rebuked herself for being foolish and tried to finish her assignment quickly. Her grandmother wanted her to go with her to the temple as she wanted to discuss something important with her. Sindhoora hoped that it was not about Akhil. She had noticed that her grandmother had seemed restless of late, especially after her discharge from the hospital.

Winding up at the office, she checked her mobile and the latest news flashed on her screen.

'A major fire has broken out in the forest near Kurangini in Theni district. There are around twenty students who were on a trek and are now trapped in the forest fire.'

****

Revathi was not willing to discuss the matter with Neel, but her husband and others insisted on it. She regarded her son thoughtfully when she stepped into his room. Neel was lounging on the couch in shorts and T-shirt working on his laptop after a wash. There was a can of drink beside him. His room was spacious, and the interiors reflected an urban and contemporary style.

"Are you busy?" She asked him and he placed his laptop on the side table.

"No mom… Why?"

"I wanted to talk to you about something important," his mother explained, and Neel looked at her inquiringly.

"Neel, what do you think of Shubashri?" She asked hesitatingly.

Neel jumped up from the couch and looked at her in anger, "Mom what is going on? Something is definitely not making sense here."

"The family wants you to marry her," she replied bluntly.

"What?" Neel was shocked. His temper rose and he raged at his mother, "Mom, has everyone gone crazy? I am not going to marry now for god's sake."

Revathi could not contain her amusement at her son's furious expression. She expected something akin to this reaction, but her sisters-in-law and father-in-law wanted her to have a word with him. They wanted to fix the alliance as soon as possible. And she was also aware that Shubashri was interested in her son.

Neel paced the room angrily. "How can you even think of an alliance without discussing it with me? Is that why dad asked me to stay back? This is not done mom…"

"Relax Neel. We will not go ahead with the alliance if you are not interested."

"Seriously mom, this is insane." And he continued his rant, "Oh, so this is the reason everyone is ganging up on me today, and asking me to go to a movie with her?"

He raked his fingers through his hair and turned back to his mother, "Mom, if this is going to be the scene, I am moving out of this house."

"Neel stop being so angry. We will not take this matter forward if you don't want to."

"Of course, I don't want to. Mom, right now I am not interested in marriage or her. PERIOD…"

"Ok Ok I get it Neel. Don't get so furious!"

Neel calmed down, acceding to his mother, "Sorry I just lost it…"

She gave a mischievous smile and replied softly, "She is not my choice too."

Neel rolled his eyes at the absurdity of it all.

14) THE ANCIENT KEY

"Without knowing the depth of the water in the tank, I struggled to come out!" Thirumurai 4 (1-5)

When Sindhoora reached home from office the next day, her grandmother was ready to go to the temple. After a quick wash, Sindhoora changed into a comfortable long skirt and T-shirt. She proceeded to the temple with her grandmother and completed the usual round of prayers and offering. There was an open *Mandapam* in the temple courtyard where many devotees were resting. Kalyani chose the other side of the courtyard, distancing themselves from the crowd. They settled down in a quiet corner on a flight of three steps. Sindhoora sat on the lowest step stretching her long skirt till her feet and resting her chin on her folded knees. In front of them was the cage where a peacock and a peahen had been housed, symbolizing the tradition that the goddess had visited the lord in the form of a peahen. The temple reminded her of her quarrel with Neel Chandra a few days ago. She sighed at her foolhardiness.

Her grandmother diverted her from the meandering thoughts, "Sindhu, I am going to tell you an old, in fact a very ancient story that my father narrated to me. Every generation in our family has passed it on to the next for many numbers of years."

Sindhoora looked at her grandmother with interest and asked, "Why didn't you tell us this story before *patti*?"

"You were young Sindhu. I wanted you to grow up and understand the importance of it. Moreover, I don't know how long I will live."

"You are going to live for many years more. Don't you want to see Adithya joining college or admire Radhi akka's baby?" Sindhoora mentioned her sister who lived with her husband in Chandigarh.

"What about your marriage? Am I not going to witness it?" Kalyani asked her granddaughter fondly adjusting her traditional nine-yard *sari*.

"Ah *Patti*! That is going to take years, but yes you will be part of that too," Sindhoora replied tongue-in-cheek and Kalyani laughed, but her sadness swept over her once more.

"What is it *Patti*? Why do you look so crestfallen?"

"I don't know Sindhu. Since coming out of the hospital, I have been feeling as if I have failed in my responsibilities in life."

"Why *Patti*? You are the smartest person I have seen."

Kalyani smiled and patted Sindhoora's cheeks, "I don't know. Anyway, I want you to hear my story carefully."

Sindhoora was aware that her grandmother was unhappy because of her youngest son's inhumanity. But she pretended ignorance, because she did not want to make her grandmother feel awkward.

She listened to her grandmother intently as she began her story, "You know Sindhoora, no one knows if any of it is a fact, but you should feel blessed that you are part of such a venerated ancient secret."

Sindhoora's curiosity spurred her to listen eagerly. The sun bid goodbye for the day and a faint flush spread across the sky above the temple. Flocks of birds flew back to their nests chirping happily as twilight descended on the city. A bright star made its solo appearance and the city welcomed the evening with glowing array of lights. Her grandmother began her story....

"Long ago there existed a pool of water called Ilamai Neerutru (Fountain of

Youth) on the deep-seated edge of the impenetrable forest of the south called Thillai Forest. It was found within the saltwaters of the Pichavaram Mangroves swamp. The pool existed at the end of a tunnel of a network of winding underground passages. Chidambaram, the city to which the pool belonged, was famous for its Lord Nataraja temple which was as ancient as Thillai Forest.

The people of the city worshipped the pool of water because of its rejuvenating and healing properties. The ancient Siddhars used the water to make elixirs. It was believed that once a year during the full moon in the month of Margazhi as per the Tamil calendar, the pool transformed into a fountain of youth and people visited from faraway lands to get a dip into the holy water. The reason behind the phenomena was that the Abishekam mixture that was performed on the lord in the temple during the full moon night and the ten days preceding it flowed through the underground channels and reached the pool of Ilamai Neerutru. Buried in the pool was a tiny golden lingam (aniconic representation of the Hindu deity Lord Shiva) No one had ever caught a sight of it but that was the belief. It was believed that the golden lingam was like an alchemist and transformed the water into a mixture of liquid that rejuvenated and healed ailments. The pool was worshipped without any disturbance during the rest of the year. This being the religious theory, there was another scientific theory for the therapeutic properties of the water. And the Siddhars came up with it."

"Who were these Siddhars?" Sindhoora asked her grandmother.

"During the Tamil Sangam Period, Siddhars were scholars who could have been saints, alchemists, mystics or doctors and they formulated a theory that the deep pool of water existed in a carved well of limestone rock which contained calcium and magnesium in abundance. The well was rich with Magnesium which was supposed to improve longevity and reproductive health. And during the Thiruvaddirai festival of Margazhi, Mercury which was considered the sacred element of Lord Shiva, was used for Abishegam and Mercury when mixed with the pool water produced the elixir. It was not known whether the water was purified later to make the concoction. Another theory that evolved was that there

was a fresh hot water spring underneath the pool, which produced the healing properties."

Her grandmother's story engrossed Sindhoora but she did not fail to notice that twilight had given way to nightfall. Her grandmother continued in her hushed tones…

"During the 6th or 7th Century, there was a legend of one of the earliest devotees of Lord Shiva, Tiru Neelakanda Nayanar. He was tested by the Lord himself for his devotion. Tiru Neelakanda was asked by the lord to dip into the pool as penance and when he and his wife dipped into the pool of water, they came up with glowing skin of the youth. Since then the pool became famous and the descendants of Neelakanda Nayanar guarded the well with profound and earnest devotion. The well was opened only during the month of Margazhi for use. One of the Siddhars recorded the healing powers of the water in their testament. They forebode that rampant abusing of the pool water would bring catastrophe to the world."

Kalyani paused taking deep breaths. She was excited to narrate the tale to her granddaughter. The oil lamps were lit in the temple and preparation for the evening *deepa aradhanai* had begun.

"So, in the year 1290 or 1295…."

"You mean in the 13th Century?" Sindhoora suggested.

"Yes, yes during the 13th Century some rulers from the north, I don't remember their names, attacked many towns in the south…"

Kalyani mused thoughtfully and Sindhoora browsed the internet in her cell phone for 13th century rulers.

"Was it Allaudin Khilji?" Sindhoora asked as the page on the ruler opened up. It was reported that his general Malik Kafur raided Central and South India.

"Yes, I think so. They started plundering Central India for wealth. Fearing their raid on temples, many of the villagers here buried the treasures and sculptures in the Western Ghats and concealed them in chambers underneath temple sites. This explanation was validated during subsequent excavations in the later centuries. So, the custodians of the Pool of healing water - Ilamai Neerutru sealed it with cover and built many levels above the pool locking each level with small gates. Five levels with five locks secured the pool from invaders and sieges. Each level had a ladder of steps. The special keys made of wood were shaped like a typical kodi maram of a Shiva temple. A small temple was built over the spot that housed the pool and a kodi maram was constructed in front of the temple. The Sentinel who guarded the pool during those years entrusted the keys to three of his four sons, treasured one himself and handed another one key to a trusted servant of his. In all, there were five keys for the gates of the pool. His youngest, that is his fourth son, stayed with him. He asked others to leave the city for different destinations. So, the three boys named after the five elements, along with their servant proceeded to Pancha bhootha sthal. They took leave of Chidambaram and settled in Srikalahasthi, Tiruvanaikaval, Kancheepuram and Tiruvannamalai respectively.

There were many onslaughts on Chidambaram temple for its treasures and many temples in the south were destroyed. In the next century, rulers of Vijayanagar Empire restored the glory back to Hindu temples. During this period many of the rulers, having heard of the pool of healing water, searched for it through the plains, mountains and plateaus of India but no one discovered it. Only the sacred texts and scriptures spoke of it."

The story was fascinating and Sindhoora listened to her grandmother with intense concentration. The night turned deeper, and the twinkling stars grew in number across the vast canvas of the sky. The *deepa aradhanai* was concluded but Sindhoora and her grandmother were seated at the same spot, lost in another world. Her grandmother continued to hold Sindhoora in her spell with her time-worn tale....

"One of the four sons called Appavan Kandan who travelled with the precious key, settled in Tiruvanaikaval. The holy shrine had underground water stream and Appu loved the town for its glory and the river Cauvery. His one treasure other than the fabled key was the musical instrument 'Vangiyam' which his father allowed him to carry. The 'Vangiyam' later came to be known as Nadaswaram and there was a period in the annals of the history of Tamil Nadu when Nadaswaram artists were the most sought after, because playing the instrument was considered to be auspicious. The later generations of Appavan Kandan grew popular with their art and travelled all over the state. When other wind and string instruments started gaining importance, the decline of Nadaswaram began and only a handful of artists continued the tradition. One of the families that continued the tradition was the progeny of Appavan Kandan. During the great famine of 1876 that affected south, a large number of agricultural labourers, handloom weavers and performing artists immigrated to other cities. The descendant of Appavan kandan had no family. He had become too aged to emigrate but the famed key that his forefathers passed on to his father remained with him. There was a belief that losing the key would entail bad omen on the family, but he had none. So, he decided to entrust the key to his best friend, a Vakil, who being a Brahmin performed religious rituals when the occasion arose and who also took care of him. So, he entrusted his musical instrument to his best friend asking him to guard both the Nadaswaram as well as the key treasured inside it very closely. After the death of his friend, the Vakil shifted from Tiruvanaikaval, but no one had any idea regarding his location, children or family."

"What happened to the other sons of the sentinel who guarded the pool?" Sindhoora asked when her grandmother took a break.

"I suppose they settled in other towns and their descendants treasured the secret."

"Hmm… so no one knows what happened to this *Vakil?*" Sindhoora asked but there was no reply from her grandmother.

Sindhoora regarded her grandmother and repeated her question, "Patti, where did the *Vakil* go?"

Her grandmother sighed and held her palms together vertically, looking at the main shrine, she closed her eyes and chanted softly, "*Neelakanda....!*"

The crowd of devotees petered out after the evening *deepa aradhanai* and Sindhoora checked her mobile for messages and mails. The evening breeze was laden with intoxicating fragrances of musk, jasmine and sandalwood, carrying with it the smell of food mixed with the odour of the crowded bazaar.

"He was my great-grandfather," Kalyani whispered jolting Sindhoora out of her senses…

****

Neel found his grandfather in the gardens, lounging on the wrought iron chair burrowed in deep thought.

"*Thatha…*"

Arunachalam jerked out of his agonising contemplation and peered at his grandson in the diminishing daylight.

"What are you doing here alone? Mahesh told me that you were searching for me earlier."

"Yes, I was…" Arunachalam sighed because it was the first time that he was lost for words.

Neel sat on a chair beside his grandfather and admired the well-maintained garden. There was a comfortable quietness in the garden.

"Nilagriva, do you remember the night that Shreekant died?"

Neel shot a look at his grandfather and nodded, "It was late evening."

"Yes, do you really think he committed suicide?" he asked as the cicadas started to make a loud shrill noise, buzzing in the garden. Neel stood up burying his hands in the pockets of his track pants as if he too was disturbed like the cicadas, "Why are you asking me this now?"

"I don't know Nilagriva. The incident which I tried to forget has risen again to haunt me."

"Why? Is it because of my presence?"

"No Nilu. Of course not! It is just that…….." he paused, words failing him to put across his thoughts.

"Do you know that I have had doubts about the nature of his death lately? And I don't think it was suicide *thatha*."

Arunachalam stared at his grandson in shock. Neel took his arms and said, "Come with me. I want to show you something." He guided his grandfather out of the garden and to his room.

****

Sindhoora frowned at her grandmother, "Who was your great-grandfather?"

"That *Vakil* who was entrusted with the key was my great-grandfather," Kalyani concluded her story and she felt as if a huge burden was lifted from her shoulder.

Sindhoora stared at her grandmother in stunned disbelief and incredulity. The revelation overwhelmed her with its sacrosanct significance.

"So, the key?" she asked in dazed wonder.

"I have treasured it for years now," her grandmother replied looking pleased with herself.

"*Patti*, are you saying that the key belonging to some ancient secret vault which was supposed to guard a pool of healing water is with you?" Sindhoora asked softly. She had difficulty in believing that something older than this ancient temple was in the possession of her grandmother.

"No, the original key shaped like a *kodi maram* was made of wood and later, over the years, it was duplicated into iron, brass and gold. I have the key that has gold covering."

Sindhoora stared at her grandmother in astonishment trying to digest the truth. She rose to her feet hastily and said, "I will be back in a minute."

She rushed into the main Sanctum Sanctorum of the temple where the Lord was represented in the form of *Lingam*. Behind the main shrine were the idols of 63 saints called *Nayanars* devoted to *Lord Shiva*. The idols rested in a row on a raised platform in the long corridor. Sindhoora perused the name of each saint and she stopped at the third idol. The name was *Tiru Neelakanda Nayanar*.....

15) THE ASTOUNDING TRUTH

"Conducts that cannot be abandoned will not hurt me…. or can they? " Thirumurai 5 (1-5)

In his room, Neel showed his grandfather the key and the note that he had received mysteriously in the post. Arunachalam studied the key that looked like the one Saraswathy showed him. He read the poem, glowering at the verse suspiciously.

"The King of the tongue was saved by the holy bull,

Even if he did a lot of misdeeds due to ignorance,

But your boy could not be saved by the evil pull,

That destroyed him due to their emergence…."

An icy fear shook him, as the underlying meaning of the verses staggered Arunachalam.

"The slave, troubled in mind, roaming around the ancient forests

Cradling the alms-bowl, craved for the poison…

Consumed by the fire with ignorance, descended down to the

End of the world, choking on struggling breath…."

Arunachalam stared at his grandson in shattering anguish and spoke very softly, almost in a whisper, "Nilagriva, someone murdered our Shreekant…"

"What makes you think so?"

"The verse…Don't you get it? Some of the words are from our ancient hymns."

"What do they mean?"

"One of the great *Shaivite* saints was known as the king of the tongue and *Nandi (the holy bull)* saved him."

"But that does not mean anything here."

"No Nilu, it means that our boy craved for something poisonous and the one who provided him with the poisonous substance has emerged powerful. Unlike the saint, Shreekant could not be saved and he was choked to death."

"Is that the meaning of the verse?"

"I assume so because some of the words are from the hymns but not in entirety."

"Someone sent it from *Cuddalore* district," Neel added, "Do you know anyone in the district."

"*Cuddalore*? There are many towns in the district, but Chidambaram is our ancestral town."

"Are any of our relatives living there now?"

Arunachalam denied and frowning, his eyes fell on the strange shaped key. He studied the shape of it and asked Neel, "Nilu where did you get this?"

"The anonymous sender had wrapped this key in the packet."

"You didn't have it in your possession earlier?"

"No."

"Nilu think hard. Have you seen a similar one before this?" Neel was reminded of the one he had found in Shreekant's room.

"Yes, I did find an identical one on the night Shreekant died. I saw it under the bed and had picked it up but then I don't remember where I had put it back."

His aunt Saraswathy entered the room stealthily and Neel noticed her only when she spoke, "I told you he is the one."

Neel grimaced at his aunt's words and his grandfather rebuked her for speaking thoughtlessly.

"What do you mean he is the one?" Neel asked confounded by their exchanges.

"Nilu, your aunt believes that the key she found in your jeans that day belonged to you."

His grandfather showed him the key that was similar to the one he received in post. It was also the same key with a tiny loop that he had found years ago on that traumatic night in Shreekant's room.

"No, it did not belong to me. I had found it in Shreekant's room and had kept it in my pocket probably."

"Didn't you come later to the room and search for it?" His aunt asked him

Neel tried to remember the events of the day, "No, when mom told me about Shreekant, I had rushed to his room to see if I could find the gift he had got for his friend that morning. When I looked down, I found this key and picked it up. I forgot about it later. When did you get this key from my jeans?"

His aunt and grandfather exchanged looks and he realised that something was going on here.

"What is going on?"

Arunachalam replied, "Your aunt saw someone who was searching for something under the bed of Shreekant on that night. When she approached the room, whoever was there had left the room. Next morning the maid found the key in your jeans while washing the clothes and she handed it to her."

"No, it was not me searching the room. I had completely forgotten about the key," Neel reiterated and watched his aunt, who was deep in thought. "What is it *athai?* You look troubled."

"So, you did not kill Shreekant?" She asked him. Neel froze incredulously at the accusation and stared at his aunt in dismay and shock.

****

Reaching home, Kalyani strode to her room and opened her trunk to look for the musical instrument. She lifted it carefully with Sindhoora's help and placed it on the floor. Sindhoora watched her grandmother bow her head in obeisance and pull out the cover from the instrument. Touching the instrument, which was more than hundred years old, with awe, Sindhoora studied the *Nadaswaram.* The main body of the instrument was made of wood and had seven finger holes and a few extra holes at the bottom. Although the body of *Nadaswaram* was built of wood, the bell-shaped bottom of the instrument was metal. Like in the case of a *trumpet, Shehnai* or *Saxophone,* a *Nadaswaram* produces sound when the player adjusts the pressure and strength of the air-flow into the pipe.

"Playing it must need a lot of strength," Sindhoora observed.

"Of course, and the sound produced is very strong, so it is played outdoors mostly. In ancient times it used to be called *Vangiyam*. According to my grandfather, Appavan Kandan had carried his *Vangiyam* from Chidambaram, while his descendants who played similar instrument called it *Nadaswaram*."

"So, are they both identical instruments?" Sindhoora asked as she observed her grandmother removing the bunched piece of cloth from the small metallic cylinder at the top of the instrument.

"It seems so. Probably *Vangiyam* evolved into *Nadaswaram* in the successive years. The structure was the same. I am not sure about the number of holes though. If you read the epic '*Silappadikaram*' you will find the instrument *Vangiyam* mentioned."

After taking out the piece of cloth, Kalyani twisted the bell-shaped bottom of the instrument and when it separated from the main body, she carefully extracted something from its cavity. It was the venerated key. Shaped like a flag staff it looked more like a souvenir than a key. Sindhoora touched it with marvel and wonder. It was supposed to be the key to a mythical pool that had existed centuries ago. It was quite heavy for a key and the image of a seated bull was welded at the top of the key.

"This is yours to treasure now Sindhu. And it has to stay in the possession of the family. My father used to say that losing the key would bring misfortunes to the family."

"But *patti*, this key does not belong to our family. So, technically the curse will only work on the family of the friend of your great-grandfather."

"*Podi Vaalu*... Anyway, store it in a safe place."

"What about the other four keys?"

"I don't know. And I am not sure if the other four keys still exist. And why do you want to know about the others? You are not going to search for the pool, are you?" Kalyani asked her granddaughter candidly. But after entrusting Sindhoora with the key, Kalyani felt relieved of the huge burden that she had carried for years. She hoped that Sindhoora would safeguard the secret like she herself had done for so many years.

"But *Patti,* there was a *Neelakanda Nayanar*. His idol is worshipped in the temple. So, the pool also could have existed."

"Maybe! And maybe not! There is no proof for such stories Sindhu."

"This key and the idol of *Neelakanda Nayanar* are evidences," Sindhoora replied and her grandmother glowered at her.

"What is this? Are you going to search for the other keys?"

"No. I was just wondering. But I promise you I will treasure it carefully."

Kalyani heaved a sigh of relief and after many days of restlessness, she slept peacefully that night.

But sleep eluded Sindhoora. She regarded the key curiously and reflected on the truth of the story. She felt dazed knowing that she owned something which had such an old and revered myth attached to it.

****

"What?" Neel asked in stunned bemusement.

"Yes! Your aunt thought that you had killed her son," Arunachalam added, regarding his daughter with growing anger.

"But how can you think like that *athai*? I was his friend and cousin. I looked up to him like my elder brother. Why didn't you ask me about it earlier?" Neel was outraged by his aunt's accusations.

"I don't know Nilu. I had wanted to ask you so many times, but you were not here. You had gone away immediately after his death. I thought you were the person who was searching for the key in that room that night. I could not believe that my Shreekant had taken his own life. I guess I wanted someone to blame." She slumped down on the chair and wept in anguish. Arunachalam instantly comforted her, unable to see her in such pain.

"*Shh* Saraswathy, it was god's decision. Do not cry dear..." Arunachalam consoled his daughter, but Neel noticed the glint of tears in his grandfather's eyes as well. Neel knelt in front of his aunt and took her hand in his,

"*Athai,* I am aware that Shreekant's decision to take his own life is tormenting you more than his death." At his words, Saraswathy flicked a startled glance at her nephew. Until now, she had never recognized Nilagriva's intuitive sensitivity regarding others' feelings. Saraswathy nodded, feeling guilty that she had suspected her own nephew to be the murderer.

"We will search for the truth; whether he committed suicide like we all assumed, or something else happened that night."

The moment Neel uttered the words; both his grandfather and aunt looked at him in shock and horror.

"Nilu we were only contemplating about it earlier," Arunachalam raised his doubt and Saraswathy stared at them in bewildered confusion.

"According to *athai,* there was someone in Shreekant's room that night searching for the key, which means that this person had been present with Shreekant earlier. And there are these cryptic messages from someone who has sent us a similar key. There was definitely something going on that night which we were not aware of." Neel looked at his aunt again and promised, "I promise you *athai* that I will unearth the cause of Shreekant's death and find the murderer."

Saraswathy brushed his hair back, tears filling her eyes once again.

Arunachalam felt the first clutch of fear at his grandson's words. A feeling of panic assailed him, but he remained quiet till his daughter left the room. The moment she was out of the door, he took hold of his grandson's arm and whispered, "Nilagriva, what do you mean that you will find the truth? Do you know how dangerous it could be? What are you going to do about it? And we are not even certain if our suspicions are valid."

"*Thatha,* we have to search for the truth, and we can't keep quiet till it is established. Don't worry I will not take any risk."

"But Nilu we are not certain if he was killed. Remember the note?"

"Exactly…do you remember the exact words of the note? And how it ended?" He asked his grandfather and when Arunachalam shook his head in denial, Neel reminded him.

"*Having enslaved myself to you, I realize you have shown my place.* Those were Shreekant's words." Neel pointed to the note that had arrived in the post, "Read these, *the slave troubled in mind roamed around the forest….*' Do you see the similarity?" Neel asked and Arunachalam exclaimed loudly, "Nilu that verse in Shreekant's note is from the ancient hymns called *Tevaraam*."

"What?" Neel asked in shock.

"Wait here." Arunachalam hurried to his room and came back with a hard-bound book. He skimmed through the pages. He paused when he found what he was looking for, "Nilu that line is taken from song-1 of *Tirumurai-7*. Exact words…"

"So, someone is hinting to us about the truth, but why would anyone remind us if he had killed him? Would they not let it rest?" Neel asked in confusion.

"Nilu, what if someone knows about the murder and trying to inform us in his own cryptic way?"

There was logic in his grandfather's words, but it seemed implausible. He studied the keys and the messages. What did the keys mean?

"Oh Nilu! those keys look like the flag masts that are constructed in *Shiva* temples. And the hymns… they too belong to the same genre. Do you think there is any connection?"

Neel could not fathom the connection between the mysterious verses and the keys. He was perplexed by the strangeness of it all. He needed to think it over with clarity. His grandfather concluded the same apparently.

"I think I will get some sleep. And Nilu don't take those accusations of your aunt to heart. She has never gotten over Shreekant's death. She has been depressed ever since."

"I know. I feel her pain. Does she know about the note?"

"No that is only between us." Arunachalam turned back to leave the room but Neel's words halted him,

"*Thatha,* do we have any business rival or an old enemy that you are aware of?"

Arunachalam frowned deeply but shook his head, "All competitors are our business rivals, but I don't think they would kill anyone for it. And I can't think of any prowling enemy. If there had been an enemy, he should have killed me first instead of my grandson."

Neel could not fault his grandfather's wisdom, but he too had his own take on it, "What if they wanted to punish you by harming your family and business?"

"Business? Is there trouble in business?"

Neel sighed and shook his head. He didn't want to cause more stress by revealing what his father had confessed. And besides, there were many discrepancies in the accounts. He needed to figure them out before voicing his concern.

Placing all the contents back into the box, Neel mulled over his aunt's accusations later that night. Did she really think that he had killed his own cousin all those years ago? No wonder she had been so cold with him all these years.

He had almost closed his eyes when the dogs barked outside. He jerked open his eyes and checked the time. It was almost 12.30, but his hounds sounded restless. He pulled the jacket on and hurried out.

In the garden, there was an eerie silence and he could not see his pets in the dark. He strode towards the gate, but the guards were stationed in their usual seats and they stood up in haste when they saw him. He walked back to the house, but some instinct compelled him to explore the courtyard around the house. He headed to the lush garden on one side of the house. At first sight, everything seemed normal, but then he heard the faint sound of keening. When his mobile flashlight flooded the garden bed, he saw his beloved Basset hound 'August' lying on one side struggling with pain.

16) THE LAND OF ANCIENT MOON

"Under his protégé, even the deprived and the forsaken found care and love. He is the supreme."   ***Thirumurai 6 (1-2)***

Neel cradled August in his arms and comforted him with soft words. He spotted Milo near his car, huddled in fear. As soon as Milo saw Neel and August, he started barking loudly and rushed towards them. There was no visible injury, but Neel realised that something had agitated them. Neel explained the symptoms to the vet, and he prescribed anti-anxiety medicines, but the doctor also advised him that distraction was the best method if it was just a momentary phase. Neel had his doubts, but he did not voice them. Someone had attacked or frightened both his hounds. Milo had been disturbed when Neel found them. He took the guards to task and contacted the agency to provide better security.

Milo and August did not leave his room that night. All his efforts to work on his laptop were thwarted by their antics. They slept in his room and by morning they were back to their usual form. The chairman of *The Bay's Architects* wanted a meeting with Neel, and he agreed to a late evening appointment. He refused to ponder the reason for the sudden excitement that the appointment had triggered in him.

Kuala Lumpur

Jeeva opened his uncle's locked apartment after many years. The caretaker had maintained it well during the intervening years. She was sad to learn that Arumugam was dead. She helped Jeeva contact his uncle's old friends. Though Arumugam's friends were aware that he had been arrested and jailed in Chennai, they were at a loss regarding the reason for such a tragedy to have befallen him. Jeeva made no progress in his aim to find the killers responsible for his uncle's death. A day before he was to leave Kuala Lumpur, he made contact with his uncle's bankers. His uncle's bank accounts needed to be terminated and the locker had to be surrendered. He did not know that his uncle had stored important documents and boxes in the locker. It was only when he came to inform the bank that they asked him to release the locker. They handed him the documents and valuables from the locker.

There were deed documents of his uncle's apartment, a few jewelry pieces for his mother and a small box with Arumugam's name written on its lid. There was an envelope attached to the box. Inside the velvet interiors of the box, nestled a key in polished gold. It had a strange shape and a tiny animal welded on one end of the key. Jeeva studied the key and rested it back in the box. He tore the envelope open and removed the stapled bunch of sheets. He started reading the contents of the sheets addressed to his uncle.

"Arumugam, my dearest nephew and my only heir to this secret.......

Intrigued by the opening line, Jeeva started reading the testimony of his grand-uncle who had bequeathed the key to Arumugam.

"As the only heir to my father, I was entrusted with this great secret that had been passed on to every generation in the family. That key you are looking at inside the box belonged to our forefathers and it dates back to the earliest century of this millennium. Our ancestors were great devotees of Lord Shiva and one of our earliest ancestors, an ardent devotee was called Neelakanda Nayanar. It is believed that he was blessed by the lord himself when he took the holy dip in the healing pool of water. Since then he had taken care of the pool. Over the years, there had been numerous attacks on the village from where we hailed, so the later generations had to close the pool and lock it up. The sentinel who guarded the pool had four sons. Each was entrusted with one of the five keys of the Pool and they migrated and settled in different destinations. Our ancestor, Theekandan,

one of the four brothers, settled down in Tiruvannamalai, a temple town near Chennai where the Lord was worshipped in the form of fire, one of the five elements. Theekandan's family passed on the key to ensuing generations. During the British Colonial era, Theekandan's progeny was a soldier fighting for the Freedom Fighter Maruthu Pandyar against the British and he was deported to Penang. He worked in Plantation and settled down in Malaysia. His next generations of children worked hard and chose to adopt Malaysia as their homeland. The key continued to be passed on and here I am, leaving the key in your hands. Arumugam, this key has been treasured for centuries and losing the key would bring misfortune to the family. So, cherish this divine gift from your ancestors and pass it on to our progeny.

When you find the missing verse of this hymn, you would know the location where the pool had existed...

"The slave, who enchanted me, lives on this land, craved by the people, for worshipping."

Your uncle...

Jeeva read the note many times but there was no mention of the village that *Neelakanda Nayanar* belonged to. Was the key the reason behind his uncle's demise? But that seemed far-fetched. He checked the map in his phone for the temple town called *Thiruvannamalai.* It was not too far from Chennai. Just a few hours of drive from the city!

He studied the other items of the locker. Nothing of importance caught his eye. He poked around the house for some clue. There were old newspapers stacked in a cupboard and an old rusted gun was found in a drawer. Arumugam had been a serving officer in the Police Force. There were some old official folders in a box that was tucked behind the row of clothes in his uncle's *Almirah.* He went through each one of them. The second last folder had the title,

"Dancing Dolls". He speculated on the meaning of the title. There were two more names of officers on the folder. He presumed that they were part of the team. Everything in the folder was mentioned in code so it appeared to be a confidential assignment. Even the *"Dancing Dolls"* was a code given to the operation. He tried to contact the other two officers with the help of the information in the folder. One of them was dead and the other had left for Australia to stay with his son. After umpteen efforts, he traced the man and spoke to him over the phone.

Jeeva was startled to learn that there had been a complex network of antique dealers across the world who used to sell the wares in the black market. His uncle and the team had investigated their network. The covert operation was called, *'Dancing Dolls'*. They had been on the verge of a major breakthrough when his uncle was asked to carry the idols discovered in the ruins of the excavations to Chennai. Subsequent to his uncle's arrest, the operation was discontinued, and no one had carried the investigation forward. Jeeva studied the pictures in the folder. There were some unique sculptures and idols recovered from various southern temples of India. With duplicates being replaced in their place in the temples, the original ones had been smuggled into the black market.

Was his uncle deceived because he had been on the verge of a major breakthrough? His uncle's colleague mentioned that black market trading of antiques had dropped in recent years. If that was the case, why was his uncle murdered after he came out of the jail?

Reflecting on all the possible conspiracy theories, Jeeva stepped out of the flat for some fresh air and dinner. He reached a popular restaurant in the city that served good Japanese food. While he was having dinner, Neel called him to enquire about his progress.

"By the way Jeeva, we received the report on your injection and the needle. The mixture of drug that was injected into you had traces of Mercury and …"

"Again Mercury? Who gets hold of so much Mercury?" Jeeva asked dubiously.

"Yes, even I fail to understand this Mercury thing. It is a banned substance except for use in medical purposes."

"Do you think some medical guy is doing all these?"

"What for?"

"Just for the kick! Sorry that is all I can come up with. My brain is in tatters today."

"I understand. What is happening with your search?"

"Nothing much! My uncle was on the verge of a major breakthrough in an operation when he was jailed."

"What was the operation?"

"Antiques smuggling…"

"Whew! That could be a reason behind the conspiracy."

"Maybe ! But why would they kill him after so many years? I believe the market for antiques is going through a rough patch. So, there was no need for them to kill him."

"And why would they be after you now?"

"Exactly! Anyway, I am here for a couple of days more. I will update you if I stumble upon something relevant."

"Cool! Take care."

"You too bro… The world is messed up. I fail to understand it anymore."

Amused at his friend's words, Neel asked in concern, "Are you drunk?"

"In the process… I would not mind if you joined me."

****

Neel disconnected the call and checked the time in Malaysia. It was two and half hours ahead of India. So, it would be nine at night. Neel hoped that Jeeva would reach Fiji without encountering more troubles. He drove to the beach and jogged for an hour. He had to cancel the late evening appointment with *The Bay's Architects* as he could not leave the meeting he was holding in one of the companies burrowed in deep financial mess. His father and uncles had attended the meeting and they were working on ways to sell the company.

He sighed as he sat on the bench after running for an hour. There were many people on the beach enjoying family time. Kids played around with sand and vendors tried to sell their edibles to the visitors. He noticed many ships anchored at the dock that lay north of the beach. He decided to jog along the coast to the spot where the ships were docked. He was aware that the area had restricted entry, but some curiosity urged him to check the place. After jogging till *Anna Memorial*, he could not go further to the Port as *Cooum River* ran perpendicular to the coast. He watched the outlet of the river dropping into the sea and noticed the glistening lights at the busy port. He decided to visit it another day and return home. While he walked back to his car, the phone call from his mother disrupted his orderly state of mind. As soon as he saw the caller identity, he presumed that she was enquiring about his whereabouts but…..

"Hello Neel?"

"Yeah mom, I am reaching home in ten minutes."

"No no Neel. I am not home."

Neel frowned and waited for his mother to continue….

"I am in *Mylapore*."

"*Mylapore?*"

"Yes, at Sindhoora's house…You remember Sindhoora? She was the one who helped me when I fainted at the auditorium."

Neel flipped out of his wits. What the hell was his mother doing at her house? And why was his mother calling him from her house?

"Are you alright mom? What are you doing in her house?"

"I came to visit her, to thank her for the other day." Neel rolled his eyes, wanting to swear at the sky, "Neel, can you pick me up from her house. Balaji had to rush home because his son got injured while playing."

Neel took a deep breath to calm his agitated nerves.

"What about Mahesh? He could pick you up. I will tell him." Neel disconnected the call before his mother could disagree with him. He did not want to go to anyone's house. Especially someone who dismissed him like he was a spoiled brat! First, he called Balaji, his mother's driver to check his status. Balaji was not answering the phone, so he called his brother.

"Hello Mahesh, where are you?"

"At the Academy. Why? What happened?"

"Nothing. Mom wants someone to pick her up. Balaji had to rush to his house for some personal crisis."

"Where is she? I could go. That is no problem. I have an hour of game then I am free," Mahesh informed Neel.

Neel sighed, "She is in *Mylapore* and she is ready to leave. I think I will go and pick her up."

"What is she doing in *Mylapore* at this hour?" Mahesh asked his brother as if Neel knew the reason for his mother's absurdity.

"I have no idea. She said she was visiting someone. And I swear I will strangle her if I found her in the house," Neel meant Sindhoora, but his brother thought otherwise.

"What? You will strangle mom for visiting someone? Have you gone mad Neel?" Mahesh had never heard Neel swearing at someone like this and he had never seen his brother losing his cool. Why did his mother's visit rattle his brother so much? He wondered…

"Oh, shut up Mahesh….."

Neel swore at every vehicle that tried to overtake him. His composure was in disarray and his mood was foul…

****

Pandayanilavur (The Land of ancient moon)

(A village near Aanamalai, Elephant Hills)

He was accorded a hero's welcome in the village. His tall and robust build commanded respect and his soothing personality invoked hero-worship. The villagers were devoted to him as if he was the Lord himself in the manifestation of a human. He travelled a lot and during the annual village festival, he returned to the hamlet to take part in the festival. Nothing in the village moved without his permission. He lorded over the village as its head and leader. His bright eyes and divine hymns beguiled the village folks into listening to him unquestioningly. They believed that he was the divine saint who would guide the villagers towards a right path. The small arc of vermillion on his forehead symbolized the Goddess Moon who was worshipped as the guiding deity of the village.

None of the villagers assimilated that the man they worshipped considered himself as the reincarnated devotee of Lord Shiva. He believed that he was one of the Nayanars who was reborn to destroy the evils of the world.

'Pandayanilavur' meaning the Land of Ancient Moon, celebrated the last full moon of the winter with glory and praise to the goddess. The festival was celebrated for a week and at the end of the first day of the festival, the villagers would pledge to avenge the families that had wronged them. One of the men whose family was sought in the name of revenge was Gangai Selvan Chettiar, grandfather of Arunachalam Chidambaram Chettiar.

17) THE ATTRACTION

"The five senses purified and induced by the beauty, the heart rejoices without a care." Thirumurai 7 (3-5)

After the late-night dinner, Jeeva was back in the apartment mulling over the life and death of his uncle. He talked to his mother over the phone and learnt the details of his uncle's trip from Kuala Lumpur to Chennai twenty-four years ago. He reflected on the fellow traveler Arumugam had taken to his hotel. The man had been found dead the next morning. Who had killed him? Should Jeeva consider talking to the man's family? Would there be any family members willing to talk about it after so many years? He had to stay in Chennai to pursue this course of action. Would he be able to discover anything pertinent that would help him expose his uncle's murderers? There were so many unanswered questions. The recent episode of poisoning indicated that someone had been stalking him in Chennai. And if he stayed there without any specific reason it would be dangerous for him. He needed a real reason to go back to the city without spurring anyone's suspicion. He could get a temporary job. He could ask Neel Chandra for a job. Yes, that is what he would do...

With that decision made, he called his mother once again to talk about his plans. He would speak to his father later because his parents were separated and his father lived in _Viti Levu_ with his new family, while his mother and he lived in _Nadi_. His mother employed a couple of workers on the plantation and he was confident that his mother would take care of the plantation in his absence.

He would ask Neel to get him a job in a pub because he was a well-known DJ in _Nadi_. Dancers enjoyed his foot tapping music and they always demanded his presence at events and functions. His weekends were never free, and his good looks attracted young women all the time. That reminded him to call his current girlfriend and update her on his travel program. There were already a couple of missed calls from her.

****

In spite of having gone only once, Neel was surprised that he could remember the directions to Sindhoora's house precisely. His mother had messaged him the plot number of the house and unlike the last time, he had no difficulty in driving into the narrow lane. This evening, there was no car in the street, and he pulled the car to a stop right in front of her house. There was a small flight of steps to the traditionally designed entrance and a pillared veranda ran on either side of the flight of steps. He rang the bell and waited in taut silence.

A boy of fifteen or sixteen opened the door and he peered at Neel in curiosity through his spectacles. Neel introduced himself.

"Neel"

"Oh yes, come in…."

The boy led Neel across the Veranda and ushered him through an arched door to the main living room. Neel hesitated and removed his shoes before crossing the threshold. He followed the boy and stopped abruptly when he sighted his mother enjoying herself with two other women in the living room. One of them, who was clad in a traditional nine-yard *sari* sat on the *Oonjal* and studied him thoughtfully, while the younger woman, who was around his mother's age, smiled at him shyly. His mother beamed in pleasure at his arrival and introduced the two women to him,

"Neel, this is Gayatri, Sindhoora's mother and that is her grandmother."

"This is Neel, my eldest son," Revathi proudly introduced him to all. The boy who had let him inside the house was hovering at the doorway, still staring at Neel with curiosity. Neel looked around the room after acknowledging the women. One of the three doors in the room led to a small courtyard which had wooden columns around it. The open roof of the courtyard provided light and ventilation in such houses. Neel presumed that the room was used for dining as he glimpsed the round table and chairs. It was a traditional house with extensive use of wood which maintained cooler temperature inside. Furnished with modern amenities and gadgets including a Wi-Fi router, wall mounted television, laptop and desk-top, the room also had many framed black and white pictures decorating the wall. His eyes, of their own volition, searched for Sindhoora.

"I hope you did not have trouble identifying the house." This was Sindhoora's mother who seemed to be the only one trying to make a polite conversation with him.

"No, I had no problem…"

The lad brought a chair for him and Neel thanked him. The women resumed their conversation as if his presence made no difference. He took the seat and hoped that Sindhoora was not at home. His phone whirred. It was his brother.

"Hi, did you reach the place?"

"Yup"

"You didn't strangle mom no?" Neel expelled his breath in exasperation at his brother's whacky sense of humour.

Neel discontinued the call and glanced at his mother. The visit had clearly enlivened his mother. Her eyes sparkled bright with enthusiasm. Sindhoora's mother handed some books to his mother and she accepted them gladly. Neel was surprised. They were behaving like old chums and their camaraderie annoyed him. He was on edge and wanted to bolt from the stifling atmosphere. And as if on cue his nerves tensed with intuitiveness. He turned to look in the direction and there she was, entering through the doorway of the dining room with a tray in her hand.

****

Sindhoora had been tense, a nervous energy had gripped her when she heard his mother speaking over the phone. She made the coffee, anticipating his arrival with a heady abstraction. She was acutely aware of the moment he entered the living room and she could hear his deep voice answering her mother's question. And the kitchen seemed too suffocating. She summoned the courage to walk through the door and took the tray of coffee to the living room. She saw him sitting across the women in his track pants and T-shirt. His thick hair was windswept lightly and his powerful arms rested on his knees casually. She could not for the life of her understand the irrational turns her thoughts were taking. But she did miss his long mane of hair. Somehow, he had seemed more approachable with his ponytail, than this short and formal hair style. And all of a sudden, he turned to look in her direction...

Their eyes met and Neel's attention was riveted on her. She acknowledged his presence with a simple nod and advanced into the room to serve coffee to his mother. He could not hold off from paying attention to every minute detail. Her head was wrapped in a wet towel and wisps of wet tendrils escaped from the loosely knotted towel. In the pale light of the room, her skin glistened and enhanced her vulnerable nape. Her snug top fitted her slender figure like a second skin and the full length of the cotton skirt heightened the allure of her long legs. When she offered him coffee, the smell of her shampoo drifted to his nostrils. Like an idiot he shook his head mutely. She straightened and the towel slipped from the top of her head and clung to the knot at the back. She placed the tray on the centre table and took position behind her mother casually. Her long arm rested on the back of the chair, her fingers clenching them tightly. Observing the faint trace of pink on her cheeks, his eyes sought hers unwittingly. The world around them froze into stillness and they felt an unknown pull which stirred their senses with the first flush of warmth. Sindhoora broke the contact hastily. His penetrating stare studied her innocent eyes, straight-edged nose and delicately pointed chin, storing them in some corner of his memory. She enticed him with her guileless charm, and he felt his pulses racing at an alarming speed. He was oblivious to his mother's presence and an overpowering urge to caress her face seized him, but the sound of laughter broke the spell and he let his eyes fall away from her. He looked at his mother who was laughing at a shared joke. His breathing steadied and his pulses slowed down. He realised that he ought to get a grip on himself. He stood up abruptly and his mother followed.

"Shall we leave, mom?"

"Yes Neel… One second. Let me finish this coffee. It is absolutely delicious," his mother uttered with pleasure and he waited, getting quite tense. He could not help but steal a glance at Sindhoora. She was holding herself rigidly in the same spot but the coldness in her eyes disconcerted him. He wanted to get out of the confined walls of the house. He felt like a tightly coiled spring.

"I am waiting outside," he informed his mother and nodded at the other women. He walked out of the house without looking back at

Sindhoora.

When he reached his car, he took deep breaths to calm his aroused senses and overwrought nerves…

****

Sindhoora deposited the tray in the sink and leaned on the wall to steady her flustered pulse. She was a quivering mass of nerves and she felt as if she had run a stretch of long distance. Neel had a disruptive effect on her and when his eyes roved over her face, she had held her nerves tightly. She had felt the heat of his stare and had flushed from their impact while she had been frozen to the spot unable to break the spell. Touching her cheek, she felt the warmth in them even now. And the strangest thing was that she had not wanted him to look away. Like a moron, she had wanted him to appreciate what he saw! And she did not approve of this new eagerness for his attention. How stupid could one get? She chided herself. Had she lost her brains? She tugged the towel from her head roughly and dried her hair with anger and self-recrimination. She closed her mind to the ceaseless image of his hooded eyes observing everything about her. She grimaced at her old faded skirt. The top was several years old and fitted too tightly on her. Remembering the chic and blonde woman who had accompanied him to the temple, she threw the towel into the bucket with aggression and stomped to her room in fury. Too many emotions were overwhelming her. Exhilarated by his presence, she felt drained after his departure. Angry that she didn't look her best, she was also disgusted at her pathetic need to want to look her best. She realised that she didn't know what she wanted. She felt confused and strung up with too many confounding emotions. Finally, she ended up falling asleep without dinner. When her father peeped inside the room, he found her curled up on the bed fast asleep. He extracted her fingers from their tight grip on the comb gently and covered her with a linen bed sheet. He switched the lights off with a fond smile and tiptoed out of the room.

****

Ponmalan lurked behind the tree in the corner of the road which housed the mansion of *'Chidambaram Illam'*. His dark figure was not visible to the security guards at the gate. He studied the security arrangements at the house very carefully. Years ago, he had broken into the house stealthily and had confronted Shreekant without anyone's knowledge, but he was not sure if he could follow the same method now. When he had tried to enter the house last night, the hounds had leapt at him ferociously, but he had managed to scare them. There were structural changes outside the building, and he needed a couple of days more to prepare for his job. He sighed and turned around to leave but his attention was caught by the arrival of a grand luxury car. Through its tinted windows he could not see the passengers in the car. While he admired the beauty of the car, it turned into the gate of *Chidambaram Illam* and its powerful tail-lights did not give him a chance to linger on the opposite side of the road. Ponmalan scratched his jaw as he strolled back to the main road, reflecting on the occupants of the car.

****

When Neel reached home, he was on the verge of physically harming someone. Such was his rage at his own irrational reaction to Sindhoora's presence at her house. He hoped that his mother had no inkling of his feelings. While he drove back, his mother talked non-stop about how she liked Sindhoora's family. They seemed to share the same likes and dislikes about music and his mother had been delighted to share her opinions with them.

"But why did you feel this sudden need to visit them? You could have talked to her over the phone and expressed your gratitude."

"I wanted to visit them Neel. These days no one has the time to attend to another person but Sindhoora not only took care of me, but also waited till you arrived. Who has the time to spare? So, I wanted to thank her personally. I am glad that I did. Her family is very sweet and welcoming. Especially her mother!"

Neel sighed! It was no use trying to convince his mother about the futility of keeping in touch with Sindhoora. He wanted his mother to break all contacts with her. He didn't want to be attracted to her and he wanted to stay away from her hypnotic allure. His cousin Shreekant had been in love with a girl and he had succumbed to the dangerous consequences of those emotions. Neel did not want to commit the same error.

So far, he had always been in relationships where he had called the shots. He had never been in a situation where he had been helplessly drawn into a relationship. And his sixth sense warned him that Sindhoora could be a danger to his peace of mind.

At dinner time, Neel found his father and uncle desperately trying to contact someone over the phone. He frowned at the urgency of their actions…

"Dad what is it?"

"It is *thatha* Neel. He is missing. He has not returned from wherever he went this morning. His phone is also switched off."

Neel got anxious at his grandfather's growing absence. Where did his grandfather disappear?

"Has he taken the car?"

"No, he took a cab."

He checked his grandfather's room. Everything was in place and in order. The servants had no idea. Arunachalam's sister Varalakshmy and her family arrived after learning about Arunachalam's absence. She berated everyone for not taking care of her brother properly. Neel's uncles headed in different directions of the city and his aunts called up their relatives to enquire.

Night was falling rapidly, and the minutes stretched to hours. Still there was no news about Arunachalam.

18) GANGAI SELVAN CHETTIAR

"As ignorant as I was, without aim, I was misguided by evil; but the Lord bestowed another chance on me." Thirumurai 4 (5-5)

Udayarajan studied the blueprint of the ten-acre ground. He would love to turn the unkempt expanse of area into a thriving resort. All he needed was Arunachalam's signature. The ten acres land belonged to the industrialist, Arunachalam and if Udayarajan acquired it he could also use the beach that ran along the edge of the ground for his other businesses. It would be like killing two birds with a single stone. He was feeling quite charged about the plan. If it worked out, he could be one of the leading businessmen in the state. His adrenaline flowed through his veins with renewed excitement.

Udayarajan did not believe the story of the healing pool that he heard during the doctor's announcement at the meeting of '*Celestial Verses*' last month. But if he did stumble upon it while burning the forests or building resorts near the wetlands, he would be happy to stake claim over it.

The landscaping project that was outsourced by Thillai Industries to *The Bay's Architects* on the outskirt of the city of Chennai was suspended due to the intervention of the young successor of Arunachalam. His sources informed him that Neel Chandra wanted to sell many of the properties that were owned by the group. It was the perfect time to pitch for the ten-acre ground in *Killai*. Udayarajan sent the drawing for copies and asked his architect to study it.

For the first time, the town of Chidambaram would have a sprawling resort with state-of-the-art amenities. Udayarajan would have to own a part of the mangroves for his resort and gain control over the three thousand acres of wetlands of *Pichavaram* slowly and steadily.

Even if Arunachalam desired to keep the ruined mansion and the wild expanse of the area, Udayarajan doubted the intentions of Arunachalam's grandson. He assumed that Neel Chandra would be happy to get rid of the land. After all, several of the enterprises of Thillai Group were running at a loss. Who would have better knowledge of it than Udayarajan?

Udayarajan could not contain the sly pleasure that his thoughts were generating in him. He had heard that the estate had thick green cover and there was a lone caretaker for the dilapidated stretch of land. What a perfect setting for his project!

He called an urgent meeting of his manager, architect and contractor.

****

Arunachalam spent the day, sitting in front of the block and staring at it. The established institution for mental illness was built many years ago and the block in front of him was named '*Ganga*' after his grandfather *Gangai Selvan Chettiar*. His grandfather had spent his last ten years in this institution and following his death; Arunachalam's father had donated money for this block to be constructed in his memory. Arunachalam did not remember his grandfather much, but the memory of one meeting many years ago at this hospital was engraved in his mind.

Usually, his father never asked him to accompany him on his visits to the hospital, but that day Arunachalam had forced his father to take him along so that he could meet his grandfather. He had no idea that his grandfather had been in the last stages of his mental illness. He had been quarantined in a separate room and he had been given two attendants. When Arunachalam had gone visiting with his father, his grandfather's health had deteriorated and the doctors, nurses and attendants had hushed meetings with his father. Arunachalam had waited outside the room impatiently for his father to finish his discussions and meet his grandfather. He must have been about eight or nine years old then.

Finally, when they proceeded to meet him, there had been tension writ large on his father's face. The nearer they approached his grandfather's room, the louder the cries had sounded. Arunachalam had been scared and he tightened his hold on his father's hands. When they peeped through the small opening in the door, Arunachalam had been shocked to find his grandfather in a terrible state. He could not remember clearly if his grandfather had been strapped but he had been on the bed and shouting angrily.

For a long time, Arunachalam could not forget the words his grandfather had uttered in rage and fear at his son and grandson. When he had questioned his father about them, his father had dismissed them as the incoherent words of a person who was unwell. Slowly time had blanked out the visit from his mind. Until now! The indelible words of his grandfather spurred his anguish once again. The death of Shreekant, the agony of his daughter, the cryptic verse of the mysterious package and the impending danger to Nilagriva on his mission to search for the culprit brought back the distant memory of the visit. It still troubled him to remember those agonized words of his grandfather…He recollected the harsh voice of *Gangai Selvan*…..

"Don't take me lightly son. They will come back to seek revenge. It may take many years and many generations, but they never forget the death of their own. They will hunt us and wreak havoc. Their goddess 'Moon' will not rest till her

son is avenged. Protect our children from their fury….Please Lord protect them. Son, are you listening to me? Run, run to safety…"

Now after many years, they haunted him. The recent spate of misfortunes that befell his family had him ruminating about the long-forgotten visit, and at the first blush of dawn, he had rushed there. He had sat there since morning in front of this block, forgetting to tell his family of his whereabouts. Somehow his grandfather's words sounded prophetic to him now and an unfamiliar fear for his children gripped him. Who was this invisible enemy trying to harm his family? When his grandfather shifted from Chidambaram to Chennai, he had joined a trading house. Later, he had branched on his own and he had built a thriving business. *Gangai Selvan* had prospered well and when his son joined him, the company had grown into a large enterprise. When Arunachalam took over the reins, it became Thillai Group of Industries. He had understood late in his life that his grandfather had lost coherency of mind steadily and gradually.

Now as the night grew deeper, Arunachalam became aware that his family would be worried about him. His phone was switched off and he had travelled by a cab in the morning. It took him some time to reach the exit gate of the sprawling campus of the hospital. Hailing a cab, he travelled back home in pensive silence. He felt an urgent need to trace the history of his grandfather. His father had not told him much about their past. If Arunachalam had to protect his family from the vengeance that his grandfather had spoken about, he had to travel back to the past and find the cause. Especially now that his grandson Nilagriva was on a mission, he needed to protect him from the evil. He would never let any kind of misfortune to fall on Nilagriva. Last night, when Nilagriva asked him if he had any business rivals, he had denied knowledge of any but when he pondered the question later, the memory of his visit to his grandfather plagued him.

****

Sindhoora had no time for lunch that afternoon. Her friends invited her to take a break, but Sindhoora had to finish the presentation by late afternoon. She was glad that she was kept busy otherwise her irrational brain would keep recollecting the smoldering gaze of Neel Chandra and his visit to her house. She was also glad that she did not have any document addressed to Thillai Group of Industries. That day she did not want to see anything remotely connected to Neel Chandra. She wanted to keep thoughts of him at bay.

An hour later, she completed her work and stretched her hands. The hall was almost empty as most of them were in the canteen for lunch. She was shutting her desktop when someone entered the hall. She looked up to find a striking middle-aged man in crisp half-sleeved white shirt and a brilliant white *Veshti*. With metal rimmed spectacles and horizontal lines of *Vibhuti* (sacred ash) on his forehead, it was a face one could not forget easily. She stood up as he approached, and he studied her before taking a look around them.

"Where are the others?"

"They are having lunch. Can I help you?" She asked him politely and he went on,

"What about you? Are you not having lunch?"

"I wanted to complete some work" She pointed at her folder.

The man, who must have been around forty years of age, smiled at her and asked her name,

"Sindhoora Vaidyanathan"

"Good! Sindhoora, have your lunch first. Then take copies of these prints and make a detailed report of the analysis mentioned here."

She was not sure of his identity, but she deduced that he was one of the senior members of the organization. She accepted them and assured him that she would get the copies ready as quickly as possible.

Once again, he studied her thoughtfully and granted her a set smile before turning back to leave.

She sighed with relief. Somehow, he had made her nervous. He had this aura of power around him. Who was he?

After lunch, she focused her mind once more on the report the man had given her. After talking to a couple of her friends in the canteen, she assumed that the man who had spoken to her was none other than the Founder himself, Mr. Udayarajan. He was stationed at the office today because of a new project that *The Bay's Architects* was getting hold of. She thanked her stars that she had not made a fool of herself in front of him.

Her eyes fell on the name of the town in the report and she caught her breath. It was the town of Chidambaram and the area of the resort that they were going to develop was located on the fringe of the mangroves. There were photographs and she regarded them carefully. Her concentration was so deep that she did not see him coming towards her and halting near her desk….

"Hi…"

His greeting jolted her out of her absorption and her face shot up at the caller. Her jaw almost dropped at the sight of the tall figure.

She was once again lost for words and he asked her, "Don't you have anything to say other than calling me names?"

"What? I have never called you names." She stood up because it was difficult to strain her neck so high to speak to him.

"No? What about punk?" he reminded her, and she wondered if he was making fun of her…

"Do you have an appointment?"

"Yes…." He checked his watch and Sindhoora was aware of a couple of officers looking at them curiously.

"Is your friend alright?" She asked him as the memory of his last visit to the office conjured up in her head.

"Yes. He is fine."

And then they stood awkwardly staring at each other. Sindhoora could not drag her eyes away from the handsome picture he made in full sleeved white shirt and grey formal trousers. And it puzzled Neel later on what prompted him to put that question to her then…

"Are you free this evening?" The words were out before he could stop them, and her eyes widened in surprise. Before she could make a sense of his question, the peon called him, and Neel followed him briskly without waiting for her reply.

Sindhoora sat down slowly, her nerves tingling after that chance meeting with Neel. What was that all about? Did he really ask her out or did she hear him wrong?

The words on the document danced in front of her and she chided her brain to concentrate on her work. She checked her attire and dismissed the passing thought resolutely. She did not care if he found her old-fashioned or clumsy. He had been to her house and Sindhoora had noted the way he had looked uncomfortable in her house. They were worlds apart and she doubted if they would have common topics to talk about …

Amidst her churning thoughts, the name *Pichavaram* leapt in front of her and she started reading the analysis on the report.

****

The peon led him to the cabin, and he met the founder of the company, Mr. Udayarajan. Balachander introduced them and Neel disliked the smug looking man at first glance. There was something about Udayarajan that rankled Neel.

"Mr. Neel Chandra, I am happy that we are able to meet each other finally. And I understand that you are not going ahead with the project on the outskirt of the city."

"No, there are things that we need to prioritize and at this moment we do not think it right to develop the property. We want to sell it and I am sorry that your efforts at landscaping have been wasted."

"It is alright. You gain some and you lose some. You have been our esteemed client and I am sure that there would be other projects that we would go aboard together."

"Sure. We are looking forward to it. So, can we go ahead by putting up the property for sale in the market? And I will send your cheque soon for the landscaping you have already done in the area."

"It is alright. Take your time. But I have something else I need to discuss with you."

Neel waited as Udayarajan dialed the number on his intercom…..

"Rajiv, get the copies of the blueprint I have given Sindhoora to make. She should be ready with them by now…"

And Neel's ears stood up on hearing her name. He was uncertain of the reason, but he resented the way the man uttered her name with such familiarity…

19) PICHAVARAM

"Fresh water fish like carp bounce in the water bordering, their scales visible to the eye…" ***Thirumurai 2 (1-9)***

Sindhoora withheld a copy of the document before handing it over to Rajiv for her own perusal later. She wanted to study it in detail because the word *Pichavaram* intrigued her. In her grandmother's mystical tale, the *Pool of healing water* was situated on the fringes of the *Pichavaram* mangroves in Chidambaram. Was there a connection between both places? She could be fanciful in her imagination, but the photographs of the dense mangroves and the green estate fascinated her. And it troubled her to learn that the chairman wanted to acquire a part of the mangroves, which bordered the estate, to develop a resort.

Her phone buzzed and she noticed that it was Akhil. She thought of ignoring it, but the persistent ring compelled her to respond.

"Hello…"

"Hello Sindhu, I am waiting outside your office."

"My office? But why?"

"Your father asked me to fetch you. Adithya was not at home so I offered to come and pick you up. It is late Sindhu. Your father was worried."

Sindhoora checked her watch and she realised that it was almost nine.

"But the client meeting with the chairman is going on still. We can't leave until the meeting gets over."

"I will wait then. I am having coffee at the restaurant opposite your office. Give me a call when you are ready to leave."

Sindhoora was reluctant to let Akhil take the trouble to go with her every time she was late. It would be unfair to him. But the long years of their friendship urged her to be more sensitive to his feelings, so she agreed to his suggestion. She could not snap out of the bond abruptly. They needed time and space to ease out of the closeness.

Mr. Pathi had given strict instructions to all that during the chairman's presence in the office, no one left until the chairman did so. That was the unopposed diktat in the office. Since Udayarajan did not appear every day in the office, the staff complied with it.

Sindhoora pondered if Neel had left or if he was part of the meeting. A few minutes later, there was some commotion in the corridor, and she guessed that the meeting had concluded. Balachander came hurrying out of the elevator followed by Pathi and two other managers. They announced a staff conference next morning at ten. Sindhoora got a glimpse of Udayarajan and Neel Chandra exiting the main door. The half-partitioned glass wall did not allow Sindhoora to take a good look at Neel. Neither did he pause to speak to her. She packed her stuff after the chairman's exit and informed Akhil.

Sindhoora lingered outside the building for Akhil to arrive. It was quite windy, and the knee-length white *kurta* and blue jeans were not enough to keep her warm. There was a nip in the air, and it made her uncomfortable. She crossed her arms and massaged herself lightly to keep herself warm. She mulled over the unpredictable weather of the city. It was unusually breezy at this time of the year. She had draped the hand printed *kalamkari* design stole around her casually and she pulled the ends of it closer while the strong gust of wind whipped her hair. She had difficulty in restraining them from straying all over her face. Her instinct warned her of being watched and she glanced around her nervously. There were many cars in the parking lot, and some had their lights on, and some were just leaving the area. She searched for Akhil. He would be bringing his two-wheeler. She stepped back as a powerful car sailed to a stop in front of her. The darkly tinted window wound down and she looked into the car.

"Want a drop?" Neel leaned from his seat and asked her. She shook her head.

"So, what are you waiting for?" he questioned.

She spotted Akhil with helmet riding over to her side, "He is dropping me," she replied. Akhil stopped beside the car and looked at them curiously.

Sindhoora hesitated for a fraction of a second because she was tempted to stand there and talk to Neel. But good sense prevailed.

She bent slightly to say "Thanks" to Neel and then moved forward to sit astride on the bike. The silver Mercedes Benz passed them as Akhil clicked the belt of the helmet in place.

"Who is he?"

"A client."

Then they rode home quietly. The traffic was heavy and at every signal, her eyes searched for a silver Benz. Did Neel really ask her if she was free that evening? She felt an intoxicating thrill at the memory of him standing in front of her desk that afternoon. She tilted her head up at the sky, but hazy clouds made it impossible to view the stars. She imagined the clouds waiting for her to glide through them to witness a spectacle. She grinned at her whimsical thought and the sensation of floating precariously on a flying object swathed her.

An *Autorikshaw* that was riding along their side played the latest hit song loudly, its lyrics kindling a kind of longing in her....

You and me,

Who compose music,

In the heart,

That reflects the dusk,

Colouring the vast sky...

Only You and me

Like a poem

We break our hearts...

Someone on the road shouted at the auto driver to reduce the volume and he smirked at him playfully. Akhil swore at the madness of the city and the traffic moved ahead as the signal turned green. None of it made any difference to Sindhoora. She was engrossed in her own world and wondered if she was walking on air. The wistful night seemed to indicate that she was on the brink of discovering something staggeringly momentous.

She was unaware that the person who was prodding her thoughts constantly was a few meters behind her at the wheel, consumed by his own feelings.

****

The luxurious interior of the car blocked the noise of the traffic and Neel was in deep introspection, listening vaguely to the song playing from the music system of the car. He could not stop speculating about the man who had accompanied Sindhoora. Who was he? Her boyfriend?

Somehow, the thought irked him. She was beautiful hence men would be vying for her attention. But boyfriend? No, that could not be. Why not Neel?

The lyrics of the next song, by a very popular band of the nineties caught his attention….

I look into your eyes

I get mesmerized

I am soaring like the eagle

Floating on the clouds

I look into your eyes

I get mesmerized

I am falling deeper and deeper

Into an abyss….

The jarring ring of his phone broke his reverie. It was his friend Jeeva.

****

Nedumaran was leaving the next day for the big city of Chennai to meet the owner of the estate he was safeguarding. He wanted to check if they had received the packet that he had mailed to them and discuss the happenings in the estate. There had been a bunch of people checking the mansion and the orchard. He wanted to inform the owners about it. Since there had not been any representatives of Thillai Industries, he assumed that no one had any knowledge of the land developers visiting the estate.

The fear that the venerated piece of land would fall into undesirable hands gripped him. He had to stop it. His forefathers would never forgive him. He had spent his whole life protecting this hallowed land of his ancestors and he would be damned if he let it slide away in the name of development.

****

So, *The Bay's Architects* were planning to develop the area into a resort. Sindhoora studied the copy of the report she had brought home. It was ten acres land that lay along the mangroves of *Pichavaram*. There was a plan to create a lake and make it a tourist attraction. Sindhoora was aghast to note that a power substation was also included in the plan. She had already learnt that the mangroves were home to some rare species of fish-eating birds. If such a project was developed, the mangroves would disappear. Dear god, this was such a disastrous project for the habitat.

She wondered if the *Pool of Healing Water* lay somewhere below this strip of land.

Was her boss aware of the ancient myth of the Pool in the mangroves? Is that why they were developing the project? Or was it just the acumen of a good businessman?

She was surprised to learn that the owner of the estate was Arunachalam Chidambaram Chettiar. Was that day's meeting with

Neel Chandra held for this project? Does that mean that *Thillai Group* had approved of the development? It galled her that the industrialist planned to sell this beautiful estate. How could they let these land grabbers step onto such a beautiful gift of nature?

She was annoyed at Neel Chandra for assigning this project to *The Bay's Architects* because she felt a strange streak of obsession for the piece of land. She extracted the key from the musical instrument and viewed it. Was it really a key to a *Pool of Healing Water*? She wanted to visit this *Pichavaram* mangrove. Her assumption that it was her duty to inform the owners about the significance of the land failed to make sense to her. It sounded like a demented fool's fanciful lore.   She was not even sure if the pool had existed in the particular area. Her extensive research on the mangroves yielded comprehensive information about the geography of the place. The mangroves covered an area of 3000 acres, and it was home to almost 175 species of birds.

Even if the Pool no longer existed in the area, she would not allow the mangroves to be ruined. She felt a peculiar connection with the region, an unknown link that bound her to it. She would discuss it with Neel Chandra. And if he did not listen, she would call on *#ChennaiWhiteKnights* to hold placards in front of the mangroves to protest against their disruption. Fronting a protest rally was nothing new to her. She had been part of the protests against building memorials on the beaches when she had been in her second year of college. And recently she had been at the forefront to remonstrate against the construction of car park over an old water tank.

She had almost finished reading the document when her friend Vidya beckoned her to the street corner. When she reached, she found Vidya waiting impatiently with a newspaper scroll.

"What is it Vidya?"

She waved the scroll in front of her and asked excitedly, "Sindhu, remember the guy we met at the auditorium? One who came to take his mother?"

Sindhoora nodded frowning at her friend. Vidya unrolled the supplement of the business edition and displayed the front-page news. Sindhoora stared at the familiar face of Neel on the picture. The headline stunned her,

"Nilagriva Chandra Shekhar – Scion of Thillai Group of Industries set to take over as the new head"

****

The moon shone like an ethereal glow on the mellowed walls of the mansion. The mild breeze swept the fallen dried leaves into a heap and a lone fox sprinted across the ground into the thick foliage. The fox hunted its prey at nights in the marshy and dank wetlands, but he also knew well that it was treacherous to venture into the mangroves during high tide. The water from the sea gushed into the channels and the currents were dangerously strong. So, he lurked in the shade provided by the dense canopy of trees and plants in the estate that bordered the mangroves. The fox rummaged among crunching twigs and snappy branches fallen during long forgotten storms. He crouched near the leaning flag staff, clawing the ground for food. Suddenly he found something shining and picked it up. It was small, round and made of metal. It was not something he would have liked to chew upon, so he tossed it aside and dug deeper into the ground. He came upon similar stuff and kicked them aside in fury. The wind was howling through the trees and he sauntered across to the broken steps of the abandoned temple and settled down to sleep. His head jerked up at the rattling sound of the door that was vibrating on its hinges. He ambled slowly to the doorway that was concealed behind the growing creepers and vines. He peeped through the gap in the hinges, but he could see nothing in the pitch darkness. He gave a long sigh and settled back on the steps as the metal coins he had tossed away near the flag mast glittered in the moonlight.

Pichavaram mangroves' covering an area of 1100 hectare is separated from the sea by a sandbar. With more than 400 water routes, the mangrove forests are permanently rooted in water. It is the second largest mangrove in the world with many rare species of plants existing in its forest. It also attracts a large number of migrant birds like egrets, pelicans and spoonbills. The channels, creeks and adjacent sea-shore provide ideal habitat for various species of birds and animals.

The locals believe that the *Pichavaram* wetlands saved them from the onslaught of the yesteryear Tsunami that devastated many coastal towns down South. The mangroves slowed the speed of the wind as it passed through them, thereby absorbing the wave energy and lowering the damage to the coastal town. Some of the locals worship the mangroves at dawn before venturing into the sea for fishing.

The land older than the existence of man had survived every disaster that nature had wreaked upon it and the powerful rays of the dawn rendered life to millions of its dwellers.

But will the mangroves withstand the havoc that man was about to unleash on it?

20) ARUNACHALAM CHIDAMBARAM CHETTIAR

"In life, in death, in suffering, in joy; you are the pillar I will never let go of." Thirumurai 3 (4-2)

Arunachalam scanned the headline with displeasure. How did these journalists gain such information? What was their source? Nilagriva had distinctly explained to the family and the board of directors that he would be helping his father and not taking over the leadership of the company like some of the directors believed. So, who was leaking this piece of information to media? His growing apprehension for the safety of his children made him uneasy. He wanted to avoid unnecessary attention of this kind on his family.

Moreover, Arunachalam was preparing to set out to his ancestral village to unearth the truth behind his grandfather's warning. He had planned to leave the next weekend so that he could tell his family in advance. No doubt, there would be objections and disapproval to his plans, but he had made up his mind. When he had gone visiting the hospital without anyone's knowledge a couple of days ago, his absence had distressed his family. His sons and grandsons had given him a set of instructions to follow while he ventured out alone. He had been amused by Nilagriva's reaction when he had told them that his mobile phone had been out of charge.

"Thatha, I can't believe that someone as intelligent as you is giving this feeble excuse," Nilagriva had voiced his disbelief even though others had not dared to do so.

"Who told you I was intelligent?" Arunachalam asked his grandson and added, "I am as irrational as my grandsons so that explains it."

His repartee had irritated Nilagriva even more.

"I am serious *thatha*. How do you expect us to learn that you had gone spitting around the hood unless you informed someone at home?"

"Spitting around the hood? What is that?" He had asked Nilagriva with a twinkle in his eyes. His younger grandson Mahesh had laughed at him and had proceeded to explain the phrase.

"*Thatha*, it means wandering around the city aimlessly, looking for adventure."

Pretending to take offense, Arunachalam had cried indignantly, "What? I was not looking for adventure. And stop using these new jargons. I don't understand them."

Nilagriva had shaken his head in exasperation.

Arunachalam had not confessed about spending the day at the hospital to his family. He had explained that he had wandered aimlessly in the city searching for a good book shop. The memory of the conversation with his grandsons creased his face with laughter lines.

He dialed the number of his old friend, who was influential enough to stop the publication from printing unwanted information.

****

The smoke drifting from the *Homam* was wafting into the house quickly and it was causing their eyes to water. Sindhoora and Adithya quickly opened all the window shutters and doors to let out the smoke.

It was their grandfather's death anniversary and the priests had assembled at the house to do the annual ritual this morning. Sindhoora had woken up early to help her mother in the kitchen and had draped a sari for the occasion. Her father had always insisted on their presence for the anniversary so Sindhoora and Adithya used to take permission of leave from school. This year, Adithya had taken permission but Sindhoora had to go to work. There was a team meeting with the chairman in the morning, so she was set to leave for office as soon as the function got over. Akhil and his family were also present, and he kept glancing at her as they observed the rites.

While the dark green *sari* in jute silk and the short sleeve printed blouse looked exquisite on her, her moderately loose side-braid and wavy sweeps highlighted her cheek bones and straight nose. She had never looked more beautiful to Akhil. He wanted to propose to her then and there in front of the family and the solemn event. He was convinced that Sindhoora would start loving him after their marriage. The love story of the characters in his favourite film '*16 Vayathinile*' *only* affirmed his belief further. He believed that if *Chappani* (his ever-green hero, Kamal Hasan played the role), the village bumpkin could make the pretty *Mayil* fall in love with him, why could he, Akhil, not do the same with his Sindhoora? With these thoughts invading his head, Akhil continued to admire Sindhoora.

The elaborate ceremony concluded, and everyone was summoned to take the blessings of the elders. As soon as the priests left, Sindhoora packed her lunch box with some of the food items.

"Sindhu wait, I will drop you at office," Akhil, who was busy, tasting some of the special savouries like *ellu urandai* and *nei appams* at the behest of her grandmother, offered.

"Thanks Akhil but I will take the auto," Sindhoora replied, closing the lid and stuffing it in her bag. Her mother packed one more box with sweets and thrust it into her bag.

"Sindhu, your office is on my way, so it is no trouble for me," Akhil insisted, irritating her.

"Sindhu, why are you refusing his offer? You will reach in time if you go with him," her grandmother endorsed his offer, annoying her further. But Sindhoora was determined to decline his offer and she got support from an unexpected quarter.

"Let her take an auto if she wants to. She is wearing *sari,* so it is safer to go in an auto than ride your bike," her father spoke quietly but in stern tones and Akhil fell silent. To her surprise, Adithya too aided her by adding, "Yes, *Appa* is right. Sindhu struggles to walk with her *sari* so an auto will get her to office in one piece."

Sindhoora made a face at her brother but she left the house with relief.

****

When Arunachalam joined the family for breakfast, he noticed that his eldest daughter-in-law Revathi, who served breakfast normally, was not seen anywhere that morning. As soon as Nilagriva joined them, he asked his father, "Dad, where is mom?"

"She is visiting the temple. I will be going to office late, so she has taken my car."

Arunachalam waited till everyone gathered for breakfast and began to put his plans into words. He had wanted Revathi also to be present too, but he would speak to her later.

The moment he announced, "I have plans to travel next weekend," almost every head on the table shot up and regarded him with curiosity.

"What plans?" His eldest son Chandra Shekhar asked him,

"I want to go to my grandfather's village."

"When did you come up with this sudden plan?" This was his younger son, Shanmugam.

"Not sudden. I have planned the trip for some time, but I have not had the time."

"How will you go? And alone?" his daughter Saraswathy questioned him. He was grateful that his younger daughter Lakshmy and her family were not staying in the same house. For the time being, he was spared from her interrogation. He sighed irritably at the barrage of questions.

"I am getting old but that does not mean that I have lost my senses," Arunachalam's retort ensued a brief reprieve from the inquisition on the table and he continued, "I appreciate your concerns, but I know what I am doing. I am taking the car and Senthil or one of the other helpers can go with me."

"Where is this village?" Finally, someone put a sensible question and he noted that it was Nilagriva.

"*Pandayanilavur* is situated on the banks of the River Amravati. It is nestled in the foothills of *Aanamalai*. I will go to Coimbatore first and then head to *Pandayanilavur*. In Coimbatore, I will stay at one of my friend's house."

"How long will you be away *appa*?" his younger daughter-in-law

Nalini enquired.

"Maybe for one week."

****

Sindhoora reached in time for the staff-meeting. She hurried to her desk and one of her co-workers complimented her loudly, "Sindhoora you look gorgeous

"Thanks Uma. When is the meeting?"

"Chairman is here already. We will assemble in the hall shortly."

The convention hall on the top floor was large enough to accommodate the entire staff. Their seminars and conferences were conducted regularly in the spacious room.

****

Everyone had almost finished their breakfast when the telephone rang. Senthil who was standing near the phone answered. He exclaimed loudly, "*Aiyya*, the car met with an accident. The one Revathi *amma* was travelling!"

Neel strode quickly and snatched the receiver from Senthil.

"Hello!"

There was pin drop silence in the room while Neel talked over the phone, "Which hospital?"

He looked at his family as they waited impatiently for him to explain, "Mom has minor bruises, but Balaji has hurt his ankle. I am leaving for the hospital." Neel grabbed the keys of the car and hurried, accompanied by Mahesh and Chandra Shekhar. Shanmugam and others followed in another car while Arunachalam and Saraswathy stayed back in the house.

****

Sindhoora and others headed to the top floor and seated themselves minutes before the Chairman's arrival. Udayarajan was as striking as the first time Sindhoora met him. His brilliant white shirt and crisp *Veshti* commanded respect. The lines of *Vibhuti* on his forehead indicated a religious person and the lean build spoke of an athletic energy. But it was his eyes that caught her attention. They were narrow and gleamed with sharpness but held no warmth. His gaze had the power to discern the mood of his listeners. In spite of his calculating eyes that reminded Sindhoora of a predator, he held everyone in his spell. She could not drag her eyes away from him. He had a magnetic allure to captivate his audience. He spoke about the sustainable projects that they were working on and praised his managers on their sincere efforts in bringing continued success to the organisation. He also spoke a few words of appreciation for the trainees and younger workers.

"And I believe the probation period for some of you is coming to an end. I have signed the reports and they are on my table. Congratulations and Best Wishes."

There was a loud applause and he continued to speak. Sindhoora recalled that her probation period too was coming to an end. She speculated the status of her training but focused her mind on the chairman's speech.

"You must be aware that we are expanding our work in other parts of the state and six months ago, we opened an office in Madurai. Now we are planning to open an office in Chidambaram because we will be developing a resort in the town. If any one of you is interested in relocating to Chidambaram, you are welcome to give your name to your head of the department. Initially, there would be only study of soil and planning. So, you can breathe easy for the first couple of months. You can even mention your areas of interest. I should have a list by this weekend." He had a brief discussion with his managers and announced, "Trainees can come to my room and collect their report. Thank you and enjoy the day."

He left and the employees huddled in groups to discuss. Sindhoora was perturbed to know that *The Bay's Architects* had acquired the estate from Thillai Group. Did it mean that Nilagriva had sold the land for development? How could he do it? Didn't he feel a sense of pride for the beautiful stretch of area?

She waited in queue for her turn to get the report from chairman. Knowing her boss Pathi, she did not expect much good from his review of her work. When her turn came, she went inside the cabin a little nervously. Balachander was sitting with the chairman and she smiled at them.

"Ms. Sindhoora Vaidyanathan, I am happy to extend my congratulations to you. Your probation comes to an end and this is the new agreement." He handed her the folder with a smile and concealing her surprise, she read the document carefully, all the while aware of Udayarajan watching her. Balachander left the room briefly and there were only the chairman and Sindhoora. The increase in her salary cheered her and she read the rules of appointment carefully before putting her signature.

"You remind me of someone I knew in the past," Udayarajan said softly and her face shot up at his comment. He gave a half-smile and sighed wistfully, "It was a long time ago. Never mind!"

Sindhoora signed the document and left the room. She frowned at the chairman's words and wondered about the identity of the person who reminded him of her. She felt restless and unable to concentrate on her work. She wanted to talk to Neel about the estate but she realised that he was not the Neel Chandra that she had understood him to be, but the heir apparent, Nilagriva Chandra Shekhar of *Thillai Group of Industries*. She was reflecting over it when her intercom buzzed.

"Sindhoora, there is someone here to meet you."

"Who?"

"He says it is a surprise."

21) NEDUMARAN VELAN

"Even after meandering like a dog without a care in the world, you took care of me; now you are everything to me and I am in your servitude." Thirumurai 7 (1-2)

Neel inspected the car. According to the driver Balaji, the car had veered out of his control suddenly and had hit a wall. Since it was mandatory for all drivers in *Chidambaram Illam* to check the cars before they take them out for the day, Balaji stated that he had examined the car thoroughly in the morning. Neel was grateful that his mother had escaped with minor bruises and Balaji with a twisted ankle.

He knelt to check the tyres. The tyres at the back were in perfect condition but the front one on the right had an indentation. He studied it carefully and checked the dent. To his shock and horror, there was a small bullet lodged in the tiny cavity. He removed it and viewed the pellet with consternation. This was not a simple case of the car going out of control.

Someone had shot the car from a distance…

But who? And why? He recalled his father mentioning about going to office late. Was his father in danger? Had the shooter aimed for his father? The car had tinted windows so the passenger could not have been visible.

He informed the Police.

****

Sindhoora stopped short as she recognized the young man who was waiting in the lobby for her. Sindhoora observed him properly for the first time. He was tall and broad shouldered with tattoos on his forearms. He had a single ring on his ear. His light eyes brightened up when he saw her.

"Hi!" he greeted her.

She smiled politely, "Hi, how are you?"

"Great" he offered her the bouquet of orchids that he had brought.

Sindhoora regarded him with uncertainty.

"This is a small token of appreciation for taking care of me when I fell sick." His explanation and his lopsided grin were appealing and Sindhoora accepted the flowers. When Sindhoora placed them on the reception desk, the girl winked at her.

"Thanks, but there was no need for it. Anyone would have done what I did."

"I know and I would have given this bouquet to anyone who did what you did that day," he quipped and Sindhoora laughed.

"So, you are completely recovered now?"

"Yes, I should thank you and Neel for the prompt action. By the way I am Jeeva," he offered his hand, expecting the same from her.

"Sindhoora."

"Sindhoora, will you have coffee with me?"

Taken aback by his question, she shook her head, "I am working. Sorry"

"How about coffee after work?"

Sindhoora studied his face for a second "You really don't have to go to such lengths to thank me. I have accepted the flowers."

"But not coffee?" he persisted

"Excuse me?" his insistence puzzled Sindhoora.

"I mean why should we not extend our acquaintance to friendship. One more friend in a new place would be helping me. Wouldn't it?" Jeeva asked her, wanting to prolong their association.

"You are new here? Where are you from Jeeva?"

"Fiji. I found a job here. So, I am trying to make new friends."

Sindhoora recollected all those warnings about strangers that she had heard since growing up. She eyed his tattoos and the single earring warily.

"Trust me, I am not shady. I swear I am a decent and nice guy." He swore by placing his right palm over his heart.

Sindhoora could not help but smile at his theatrics and his entreating eyes changed her mind.

"Ok, just coffee! There is a coffee shop across this road."

"Great! What time?"

"We have tea break at six."

"Awesome and thanks Sindhoora for accepting my invitation."

Sindhoora smiled, wondering whether she was doing the right thing. The receptionist gave her a thumbs-up. Sindhoora went back to work concluding that he should be decent enough if he was Neel's friend.

****

Arunachalam could not forget the words of his son, "*I will be going late to office, so she has taken my car.*" Did Revathi bear the brunt of danger meant for his son? He looked at the portrait of his wife and asked her silently, "What is happening to our children? Why is danger lurking around them?"

The enemy was in the vicinity and threat loomed over his family. His grandfather's words haunted him, and he closed his eyes and prayed silently, "*Neelakanta*, if something happened to any member of my family, I would not be able to take it."

"*Aiyya*, there is someone to see you," Senthil's message roused him from his commune with the Supreme. He felt as if the Lord was responding to his prayer. Arunachalam met his visitor and he was surprised to find a familiar face that crinkled with smile at the sight of Arunachalam.

"*Nedumaran* what are you doing here?" Arunachalam recognized the old bearded man as the manager who took care of the estate in Chidambaram.

"How are you? I wanted to discuss something important so I thought I will come to Chennai and meet you in person."

Arunachalam remembered the packet and the key. He exclaimed, "My god Nedumaran! It was you who sent the packet to Chandra Shekhar."

"Yes, and I didn't get any response."

"Come, let us sit in my room and discuss," Arunachalam took Nedumaran to his room and Senthil who brought the tray of coffee scowled at their departing backs.

****

Jeeva Velu Stane arrived at Sindhoora's office at 6 pm sharp and waited for her. Restless energy seized him, and he wanted to make a good impression on her. With his jeans and white stringed cotton jacket, he knew he looked casual and smart. Even the pretty receptionist was bestowing him with admiring looks.

Sindhoora greeted him as he was viewing the framed landscape on the wall, "Hi!"

"Shall we go?" Jeeva asked trying to hide his excitement at her presence. Dressed in the same *sari* that she had worn earlier; her hair was braided in loose knots. The oxidized earrings dangled against her jaw as they walked across the road. He was acutely aware of her nearness and her perfume.

They ordered coffee, Filter for Sindhoora and Cappuccino for Jeeva and settled at the table along the window.

The peppy song that was playing added charm to the ambience and Jeeva could not help but gaze at Sindhoora's heart-shaped face. The wide attractive eyes hinted innocence and their warmth added to the allure. The dark curling lashes enhanced the softness of her face and the straight nose made it exquisite. She looked up from the menu card and he flushed. Strangely, he was tongue-tied.

"So, where do you work?" Sindhoora asked him and his reply surprised her.

"I work as DJ at the *Rhythm & Sounds,*" he named the most popular pub at one of the luxury hotels of the city.

"Oh!"

"Yeah and at Fiji I was taking care of our Plantation during the week and at weekends I was the sought-after DJ," he explained, aware that he was trying to impress her.

"What plantation?"

The coffee arrived and the half an hour flew by. Sindhoora checked her watch and realised that she had to get back to office.

"I should leave now."

Jeeva realised that he had been the one doing most of the talking. She had not revealed anything much about herself.

"You are a good listener. I have never talked so much about myself to anyone on the first date."

Was this a date? She frowned at his choice of words. They walked back to the office, each deep in thought. When they reached the office, Sindhoora thanked him for the coffee.

"Can I see you tomorrow?" Jeeva asked her, not wanting to let go of her.

"I don't think so," Sindhoora turned down his request politely.

"How about day after tomorrow then?" Jeeva could be dogged when he wanted.

"Sorry, I am not free."

"Whoa, you do play hard uh?" Jeeva exclaimed not used to women turning him down.

That annoyed her extremely and she lost her cool. The jerk! Did he really think that she was playing hard to get?

"You said you wanted to make friends, so I agreed for coffee. Now that I know that you think, that I am playing hard to get, I am certainly not interested in being friends with you. Bye Jeeva." She walked away in irritation, wanting to shove the flowers back at him. But good manners prevented her from being too rude.

Jeeva stared after her, berating himself for being foolish. He sighed. That definitely didn't go right. He had been an over-confident ass. He looked at the amused receptionist who grinned at him with mischief lurking in her eyes.

"You are wooing the wrong girl," she told him softly.

"Am I?" he asked with a flirtatious smile.

"Yes! She is not single. She has a boyfriend," the receptionist replied, and he felt his spirit going down.

So much for his efforts! No wonder she got angry. What a fool he was!

****

Arunachalam and Nedumaran discussed the purpose of his visit and Nedumaran explained how he wanted to caution them about Shreekant's mysterious death.

"What do these verses mean? And that key?" Arunachalam asked Nedumaran after they had coffee.

"Let me explain it in detail Arunachalam. Your grandson did not commit suicide. I believe he was killed."

Arunachalam was aghast. Though he and Neel had doubts, it was appalling to hear the truth spoken so bluntly.

"How can you be so sure of it?"

"I have seen your grandson a couple of times in Chidambaram. He used to come in search of the addictive substance. Initially I didn't know that he hailed from your family, but later when I met him, he told me who he was. I tried to dissuade him from the addiction, but he was beyond control. Then I heard that he had taken an overdose and killed himself."

Arunachalam listened to him carefully even as his old wounds reopened. He still remembered the gut-wrenching moment when he had found his grandson dead.

"Arunachalam I need to share an old secret of mine. It is too precious to discuss over the phone or letter."

"What is it Nedumaran?"

"Your estate land is very ancient and sacred. There is a belief that somewhere near your estate, there was a pool that had healing water. It was called *'Ilamai Neerutru'*. Some called the water elixir, and some spoke about it as the healing tonic. Over the centuries, there have been rulers and explorers in search of it. It has also been mentioned in some scriptures of *Siddhars*."

Senthil entered with the tray of coffee and Nedumaran fell silent. He waited till Senthil left them alone and then closing the door; he made sure that no one was listening to them. He lowered his voice and whispered, "Arunachalam, have you heard of the *Nayanar, Tiru Neelakandan*?" When Arunachalam nodded, Nedumaran continued, "You must have heard of his story in *Thirumurai*. You remember the Pool of Healing Water in the story?"

Arunachalam nodded thoughtfully, trying to remember the ancient tale of the venerated *Nayanar*.

"The pool where he took the holy dip as penance for his sin is the one I am talking about. There is a possibility that it is buried somewhere in the estate."

What he heard was so astonishing that Arunachalam could not speak for a few minutes. Blown away by the staggering revelation about his ancestral land, Arunachalam stared at him in confusion.

"*Neelakanda Nayanar* was my earliest ancestor," Nedumaran

declared with pride and Arunachalam gazed at his visitor with awe. How did he spend his eighty-three years without the knowledge of such a divine truth?

"Nedumaran, are you saying that the famous pool lay in that estate?"

"Yes, but it is not accessible. During the 12th or 13th century, one of my ancestors concealed the pool with many structures above and locked them up. He entrusted the keys to his sons."

Nedumaran continued as Arunachalam listened to him in keen earnestness.

"Like the one I sent you, there were five keys to the five floors of the structure. His three sons and a trusted caretaker carried one key each to the *Pancha bootha sthalam*. One key remained in Chidambaram with one brother. I got the key from the descendants of the brother who stayed in Chidambaram and since I don't have any family, my father asked me to hand it over to the owner of the estate."

"Is that the reason you sent the key to us?" Arunachalam asked, "But what is its link to my grandson's death?"

"Powerful people are searching for the keys. And I think they believe that your family has one of the keys."

"There was an identical key in Shreekant's room on the night he died."

"See, I told you! Someone is searching for all the keys to the Pool," Nedumaran mused aloud.

"But the location of the pool is a mystery. How would anyone know that it was situated in the estate?"

"The descendants of the brothers would know about it, like I know!"

"Hmm it makes sense," Arunachalam reflected. Then as an afterthought he asked Nedumaran, "You said you had tried to dissuade Shreekant from his addiction but how did you know he was addicted?"

Nedumaran looked at him sheepishly and replied, "I come across the same dealer for my hash occasionally."

"Dear Lord! At this age?"

Nedumaran laughed at Arunachalam's reaction, "What has age got to do with it? Even the ancient sages relished it. I am a slave of the Lord and it emancipates me from his slavery. Remember the song of Thirumurai-7?"

"Never letting go of you in my thoughts,

Always in your servitude, I cannot deny that

I was once lost like a dog but with your grace

I found my place…"

Arunachalam liked Nedumaran, the old rascal. He was an interesting character and in spite of their ages being similar, their outlook on life was different.

"Now that I have unburdened the truth to you, I think it is time for me to travel. I won't be able to take care of the estate. And one more thing! There are developers scouting the estate. You need to stop it. It is sacred land. Take care of it. I have entrusted you with my key. Do not let it go out of your family. Losing it will bring misfortune to the family," Nedumaran warned Arunachalam.

"Thank you for revealing the truth to me. My grandson Neel will cherish the key, but I still think that it should rest in your hands as you are the rightful owner. And the land should be owned by you, not me."

"No no, Arunachalam, your children have the right to the estate. Ask them to treasure it. It is a blessed piece of land. Do not lose it."

Nedumaran was taking leave of Arunachalam when the main door of the house opened, and a middle-aged couple entered.

Nedumaran stared at the woman in shock. It was the same face which had haunted him for years. The woman with the divine voice whom he had worshipped for decades!

22) THE UNKNOWN FOE

"Evil can never come close to the divine feet, and those suffering who seek him with true intentions will be protected." Thirumurai 6 (6-2)

Nedumaran stared at the woman with shock and incredulity. Had his destiny created a wonderful serendipity? He had assumed that he would never find her again, but he supposed that his fate was humoring him. She looked more delicate now than she had twenty-eight years ago. Slightly older, she had retained the grace and elegance. He noticed the bruise on her forehead and arms. He frowned and glared at her husband. Meanwhile Arunachalam took pride in introducing his children to him.

"Nedumaran, this is my son Chandra Shekhar, his wife Revathi and my grandson Mahesh. Chandra, Revathi, this is Nedumaran. He takes care of our estate in Chidambaram."

Acknowledging them, Nedumaran was more concerned about Revathi's bruises, "How did you get hurt?" he put the question to her politely. Her husband replied, "The car she was travelling in skidded out of control."

"How is Balaji?" Arunachalam asked his son.

"He hurt his ankle but otherwise he seems fine."

"And Nilagriva?"

"He is following us. Come Revathi..." He guided his wife out of the room and Arunachalam asked his grandson, "Mahesh, how did the car skid out of control?"

Mahesh regarded Nedumaran with hesitation before replying,

"When Neel checked the car, there was a small bullet lodged in one of the tyres."

The blood drained from Arunachalam's face and a chill ran down Nedumaran's spine. Shock paralyzed them, "Bullet? You mean someone shot at the car?" Arunachalam asked in fear.

"Yes. Neel is with police, trying to probe into the matter." Mahesh noticed his grandfather's pale face and tried to comfort him, "*Thatha*, do not worry. We will sort it out soon."

Arunachalam slumped down on the sofa. Nedumaran and Mahesh noticed his pallor. Mahesh hurried for a glass of water and Nedumaran held Arunachalam's shoulder, "Arunachalam, are you alright?"

Arunachalam nodded but fear consumed him, "Nedumaran don't you see that they have started attacking my family?"

"Who?"

"I don't know. An unknown enemy! They are going to destroy my family." He looked up at Nedumaran and asked, "You were saying earlier that there are powerful people hunting for the keys?"

"Yes, but they have been searching for the key for a number of years."

"You said they might have killed Shreekant for it. Didn't you?"

"Yes, I think they did. They probably thought that he owned one of the keys."

"I don't want the keys Nedumaran. You take them back. If it is going to endanger my family then I don't have the right to own them."

"What keys?"

Neel's sudden appearance startled Nedumaran and Arunachalam. "You were saying something about the keys endangering the family." Neel probed, glancing at Nedumaran and his grandfather skeptically.

"Nilagriva, this is Nedumaran. He is the one who sent the packet from Chidambaram. He is the manager of our estate. And Nedumaran, this is Nilagriva Chandra Shekhar, my eldest grandson."

Nedumaran studied Nilagriva curiously. He presumed that he was Revathi's eldest son. There was an uncanny resemblance between mother and son. Nedumaran's wise eyes discerned an inbred strength of character in the boy's personality. Shreekant had been a slave to his vices, but he didn't think Nilagriva would succumb to such venality. Nilagriva's eyes spoke of courage and an innate ability to take charge. He exuded positive energy. Nedumaran smiled warmly at Nilagriva as he appreciated this meet with Nilagriva Chandra Shekhar, *the blue moon hero.*

Neel was surprised that the lean old man who looked more like a sage than a manager, was the one who had sent the packet from Chidambaram. The man's eyes revealed deep insight and sharp wisdom. His long white beard, unkempt hair and an apparent commitment to his duties indicated an altruistic person. Neel gathered that the old man personified a powerful blend of adherence to tradition and a relentless pursuit of truth. Arunachalam added, "Nedumaran, the estate belongs to him and he is the heir to my business empire."

Nedumaran understood what Arunachalam was trying to imply and acknowledged it silently.

"That mysterious packet you sent; shall we discuss it?" Neel interrupted their train of thoughts and Arunachalam replied, "We have already discussed it. He was leaving just now."

"Where are you staying?" Neel asked Nedumaran,

"Not yet decided. I was thinking of resting at the waiting room in the station."

"Were you planning to go somewhere?"

"Don't know. I may return to Chidambaram."

"Why don't you stay in Chennai for some more days? There is a guest house behind this building. You can rest there for a couple of days," Neel offered and his grandson's hospitality surprised Arunachalam.

Nedumaran reflected over Nilagriva's offer. He could recognize that the boy wanted to talk about his cousin and the key. As he did not mind spending time with Nilagriva, he accepted the offer and accompanied Neel to the outhouse.

****

The rattling sound of the train disrupted his concentration and he grimaced at the noise. The midday heat was growing warmer and the paddy fields swayed in the balmy breeze. From the open Verandah of his bungalow, he could view the fields basking in the sun and the workers bent over the crops. The rolling hills of Aanamalai rose above the horizon. Gazing at the hills, he had often wondered about the name that the hills had acquired. Aanamalai which meant 'Elephant Hills' was named after the animal due to the shape of the hills, but he found no similarity between the hills and the animal.

Nestled in the foothills of Aanamalai Hills was the village called 'Pandayanilavur' meaning 'the land of the ancient moon'. One of the tributaries of River Kaveri, the river Amaravati flowed through this village and there was a belief that the warrior Goddess Durga, who in the form of a Full Moon, bestowed her blessings on the villagers on the full moon night of the month of Panguni, the concluding month of the Tamil Calendar. On a clear winter night which was very rare in Pandayanilavur, the reflection of the full moon could be viewed on the flowing waters of the river and the sight of the reflection on that particular full moon night was considered very auspicious by the villagers. Often, when the festival of the Full moon neared, clouds and mist from the dense forest shadowed the moon thus making it impossible for the villagers to view its reflection distinctly. It was also believed that on that night of the year when the full moon reflected clearly on the river, the Goddess Moon blessed her favourite devotee with wealth and happiness. There was a temple built for the Goddess Vanadurga on the banks of the river.

A small village with just seventy to eight families earning their livelihood through agriculture, Pandayanilavur had become famous for its undiscovered treasures hidden in the deep forest. During 12th and 13th Centuries when invaders plundered the temples, villagers from temple towns had hidden the treasures and precious idols in the Western Ghats, part of it being Aanaimalai Hills. So, on one full moon night, a villager had stumbled upon a precious idol. Since then, Pandayanilavur was hunted and searched by Archaeological departments, international excavation teams, and bounty hunters.

History has been a witness to many downfalls of dynasties and empires but not many realize that the beginning to the end starts with its gullible subjects. The villagers of Pandayanilavur accorded obsessive reverence to superstitions and myths. It depended on men like him to gain benefit from such age-old credence. He was not a native of this village. He had arrived here on a dark moonless night with blisters and wounds on his feet. The villagers had healed his wounds and had taken care of him. When he had realised that he was on the Land of the Ancient Moon, he had decided to stay back. Since then he had dedicated a part of his life to the welfare of the villagers. Other than meditation, he indulged in pottery, donating the wares he made to the villagers free of cost. In the evenings, he would sing verses from the famous Tevaaram to his ardent followers in the temple, situated by the river where Lord Shiva was also worshipped in the form of a lingam.

Wasn't it the English Poet Chaucer who said, "Strike while the iron is hot"? He was going to strike really hard at a time when it was least expected.

Someone knocked on the door and he looked up at the young man, who entered.

"Vanakkam aiyya!"

"Vanakkam Manickam! What is the news you have?"

"Our man is sighted, and he has made his first attempt."

"Good, I am happy to hear it."

"Aiyya the vehicle is here. Do you want to travel into the forest today? There are clouds gathering and if we don't come back by evening, we will get stuck in the forest."

"Don't worry Manickam. We can make an attempt. Come, let us leave right away. Ask Raja also to join us."

Once a week, he would travel to the forest with his men to explore for site to build his dream project. In truth, he was in search of the mythical body of water in the thick forest surrounding the river and hills. It had become an obsession for him to find it. Since the time he had read the century old book, he felt destined to discover the pool. He believed that the earliest Nayanar had reincarnated in him and it was his Karma to search for the Pool, hallowed by the Nayanar and later worshipped by his followers. The movement started by the faction to restore *the faith of the followers of Nayanars had gained momentum after the initiation of more members. He believed that his relationship with the Blue Moon God was time-worn and that he was reborn to recreate the feverish faith of the followers through the ideologies of the ancient verses. And to fulfil his dream, he needed to obtain the keys and rediscover the healing pool. By revealing the existence of the Pool called 'Ilamai neerutru' of Tiru Neelakanda Nayanar, his Blue Moon God would soon be accepted as the Supreme in the world.*

****

Assuring himself that Nedumaran was comfortable, Neel decided to talk to him the next day after the old man had a good night of sleep and rest but Nedumaran had other ideas.

"What is it you want to talk to me Nilagriva?"

"Everyone calls me Neel."

"But your grandfather addresses you as Nilagriva so I will follow him."

"What did you mean in the verse about the slave being choked to death? Has it got anything to do with my cousin Shreekant?"

Nedumaran sighed and stretched his tired body. He watched the handsome boy and smiled at his restlessness.

"Do you know that your cousin had been a drug addict?"

Neel nodded and he continued, "He used to come to Chidambaram for it. You may not know it, but one can get the forbidden substance easily and cheaply in the outskirts of the town because the stuff is unloaded at the beach and transported illegally to all places."

"Do you use them?" Neel asked intuitively and Nedumaran

affirmed Neel's doubt.

"I use them occasionally, but I always knew the limit. Kids like Shreekant though were hooked to it. Once, we chanced upon each other while waiting for its delivery. I was shocked to see the addiction in a boy hailing from this reputed family. I took him for lunch and advised him on its adverse effects."

"How did you know that he belonged to this family?"

"I asked him once when he had travelled from Coimbatore during vacations."

Neel's uncle, i.e. Shreekant's father, used to live in Coimbatore with his parents. His aunt Saraswathy also stayed in Coimbatore until the death of her husband.

"But the boy was beyond caring. He lived for the thrill and ecstasy. He once told me that in Chennai, he had befriended a man who provided him drugs at a specific place. But when the man failed to appear, Shreekant would come to Chidambaram to buy it."

"Do you know the name of the man or the place Shreekant used to meet him?"

"His name was Ponmalan and I know that Shreekant used to meet him in *Mahabalipuram*. There were always a bunch of kids searching for narcotics and they used to throng this medieval city. In the haven of the ancient shore town, there was another covert lifestyle where travelers, young men and women swayed in ecstasy under the influence of these drugs."

"And you think Shreekant was killed for drugs?"

"I think Shreekant was killed for something else."

"For something else?"

"Yes, Shreekant used to run out of money for drugs. He used to steal jewelry and money from his grandfather's house in Coimbatore as well as Chennai. One day, he showed me a gold key that was very similar to the one I had. The sight of the identical key of a very rare kind worried me. When I asked him, he said he had stolen it from the guy who provided him drugs."

Shreekant's desperation appalled Neel. He had not been aware that his cousin brother's life depended on the drugs.

"So, you think the guy had come back to retrieve his key?"

"Yes, and I am sure that he was the one who killed Shreekant."

"What is so special about these keys? You say you have a similar one. You sent that key in the parcel, didn't you?" Neel enquired

"Yes. It is a long story."

Neel took a seat as Nedumaran began to narrate.

"There are only five keys like these. Do you want to hear the story? It is a long and old one."

23) THE POOL OF HEALING WATER

"Even the glory of the rising sun from the east fades into the west, the fledgling blossoms but withers; nothing lasts except the supreme devotion." Thirumurai 10 (7-1)

"There are five identical keys and they belong to a vanished world where natural resources were worshipped as divine gifts from the Lord himself. Do you know Nilagriva; in a strange paradox, man obliterates the very same treasure that enriched him. As long as it is beneficial, he would revere it and then he ceases to care about it."

Neel waited patiently for Nedumaran to go ahead with the story of the keys.

"So, coming back to the keys, they are the gateway to a *'Pool of water'* that has been searched by one and all for centuries."

"What is so special about this *Pool of water*?" Neel asked

"People worshipped this pool of water called *'Ilamai Neerutru'* for its rejuvenating and healing properties. The ancient saints used the water to make medicines and elixirs. One of the earliest devotees of Lord Shiva, *Tiru Neelakanda Nayanar* was tested by the Lord himself for his devotion. The Lord asked *Neelakanda* to take a dip into the pool as penance and when he and his wife plunged into the pool, they emerged out of it with glowing skin of the youth. The pool became famous due to the miracle and the following descendants of *Neelakanda Nayanar* guarded it with utmost devotion."

Neel failed to understand the significance of something that was revered so long ago. What did it have to do with the present? But he did not voice his thoughts aloud. Nedumaran continued with his narration, "So when rulers from North started raiding and invading our towns, my ancestors, that is the custodians of the *Pool of Healing*

Water, sealed it."

"Your ancestors?"

"Yes, *Tiru Neelakanda Nayanar* was my earliest ancestor," Nedumaran revealed with pride once again and continued with the story. "They sealed the pool by building five structures above it and locked the door of each floor with a key that was similar to the one I sent you. The five keys owned by the brothers and a servant were passed on to the succeeding generations. Many scholars, explorers, kings and rulers have searched for the Pool through the plains, plateaus and mountains of India, but no one had discovered it. Only the families of the brothers and their subsequent generations had knowledge of it. One of the brothers stayed back at Chidambaram with the key. He passed on the key to his offspring. And thus, each generation continued with the tradition. I received the key from my father."-

"Have you seen this body of water?" Neel asked Nedumaran

"No."

"Do you know where it was?"

"According to legend, it was found within the saltwater of *Pichavaram mangroves swamp.* The pool existed at the end of a tunnel, which was a part of a network of winding underground passages. *Chidambaram, Thillai forest & Pichavaram* are cited in some of the ancient hymns."

Neel had no idea what the man was talking about. He was concerned only about his cousin's death. He was not even aware that there was an ancestral mansion on the estate in his father's hometown.

"So, if Shreekant stole the key from the drug dealer, that guy could have been one of the owners of the key," Neel suggested thoughtfully.

"He could be, but I can't believe that a drug dealer owned something so valuable."

"Do you really believe that these keys belong to a bygone era? It could simply be a story spun by some fool."

"And I suppose that fool is me or my father or my grandfather," Nedumaran asked sardonically.

"I didn't mean it that way."

"No, you youngsters only believe stories that are spoon fed to you by Westerners. You can't come to terms with local legends and beliefs."

Neel could not help but smile at the way Nedumaran rebuked his generation.

"Look Nilagriva, whether you believe it or not, the truth is that there are people searching desperately for the keys. And there are vultures hovering over the area. You have to hold on to that piece of land very strongly."

"What vultures?"

"Builders! For last two weeks, there have been teams visiting your estate and discussing plans to convert it into resort. I travelled to Chennai urgently to warn your family against allowing strangers or builders on the area. The families who own the keys should hold on to the land."

"What is so special about that land?"

"Don't you get it Nilagriva? That pool we are talking about is underneath that estate somewhere."

Neel stared at Nedumaran with dawning comprehension.

"Nilagriva, people believed that once a year during the full moon of the month of *Margazhi*, the water transformed into a pool of healing water and they visited from faraway lands to get a dip into the healing water. The reason behind the phenomena was that the *Abhishegam* mixture from the temple during the full moon, and the ten days preceding it, flowed through the underground channels and reached the pool of *Ilamai Neerutru*. Buried in the pool was a tiny golden *lingam*. No one has caught a sight of it, but it was believed that the gold *lingam* was like an alchemist and transformed the water into a mixture of liquid that rejuvenated and healed ailments. The Pool was worshipped without any disturbance during the rest of the year. "

"Are you saying that this sacred Pool existed in our family estate?"

"Precisely! There was another scientific theory for the therapeutic properties of the water. The deep pool of water was carved out of a well of limestone rock which was rich in calcium and magnesium. Magnesium which was supposed to improve longevity and reproductive health was present in large quantities in the well. It was not known whether the water was purified later to make the concoction. Another theory that evolved was that there was a fresh water hot spring underneath the Pool which produced the healing properties. It was locked and sealed by my forefathers. During later centuries, they sold the estate to your family. The five keys are proofs of its existence."

"You stay in the estate. Don't you know where it existed?"

"No. I have not ventured deep into the estate. I have not explored the dense forest. I only looked after the mansion which served as a guest house."

 "What if, one of the owners of the keys, wants to reopen the gates of the pool?"

"Then you have to stop it Nilagriva. The pool is sacred. Debasing it will bring catastrophe to the world."

"This tank or Pool that you are talking about existed centuries ago. It could have vanished considering the environmental changes."

"Yes, like you say the Pool could have vanished, but we need to let the bygones be bygones and not try to delve into it," Nedumaran replied thoughtfully.

"So, who are these people trying to search for it and why would they try to harm my family?"

"The man who killed Shreekant could have been one of the descendants of the brothers and wanted to learn the existence of the pool or he could have just killed your cousin to exact revenge for losing the key to him."

"It does not seem convincing enough a motive to kill someone. Are you sure that Shreekant was killed?"

"Yes, because rediscovering the Pool or the land surrounding it would bring immeasurable wealth. And the key is the gateway to the Pool."

Nedumaran dug into his cloth bag and tried to retrieve something.

Finding it, he sighed with relief. He extracted a small pouch made of silk and loosened the string of the pouch. Inside the pouch were two coins. He showed them to Neel.

"I found these ancient coins in the estate."

The coins glinted in the light and Neel realised that they were gold.

Nedumaran explained, "They are from the *Chola dynasty* period. I found them on the ground and if we start excavating the place, we might come across unexplored treasures. But we will not."

"Why not?"

"Because we have to protect our natural resource! The estate borders the mangroves and if we start digging the land for buried treasures, the mangroves would disappear resulting in erosion. Moreover, ancient texts have mentioned that we have to preserve the Pool, and no one should use it for worldly acquisitions."

Senthil brought a plate of food for Nedumaran and Neel left the old man alone with his thoughts and beliefs. What perturbed Neel more was his cousin's addiction and desperation.

How could Shreekant be so depended on that stuff? How did he get into the habit? Had Shreekant been depressed?

Many thoughts clamored for answers. Neel decided to drive through the route that his mother had travelled that morning. He had learnt from Balaji the exact spot when the car had gone out of control. He stepped off the car to study the scene. It was not a very busy road. There were institutions on one side of the road and on the other side, there was a park. So, if someone had shot the car, he had to have shot from one of the buildings of the institutions. As he stood analyzing the area, the police officer who was investigating the incident, asked him to come to the station immediately. The sun was setting for the day, so he hurried to the Police station before it got too late.

****

Ponmalan waited for the right moment to sneak into the house. The guards would go for dinner break in a few minutes and he would enter through the wicket gate of the garden quietly. As he lurked behind tree, the man he was waiting for came out of *Chidambaram Illam* and met him, "He is staying in the outhouse. Do your work quietly and be quick."

Ponmalan was let inside the compound of the house through the side gate and he hid his face with the hood. He walked stealthily towards the house. He sighed with relief when he did not find the hounds. He hated them.

****

After the meals, Nedumaran stretched on the bed but sleep eluded him. He was staring at the ceiling when he felt the uneasiness in his stomach. He massaged his unsettled abdomen. He realised that the food he ate had unnerved his system. He checked the plate with leftovers and arrived at an instinctive conclusion that someone had mixed either poison or toxin in the food. He started feeling giddy. He rushed to the bathroom and wetted the soap. He checked if he could use the wet soap for the purpose he was searching for. He scrawled on the back of the door with the soap and went back to sleep on the couch.

Ponmalan entered through the window and treaded softly towards the man. He masked the man's face with the bed sheet. Quickly and efficiently, he hauled the man on his shoulder and exited the house without encountering anyone. After dumping him on the back seat of his van, he sped away and planned his exit from the city at late night.

****

Neel studied the report at the Police Station. The bullet that pierced into the tyre was fired from a short recoil-operated semi-automatic pistol.

"So, any idea about the weapon owner?" Neel asked the Police officer.

"The pistol is not produced in India."

"No?"

"No, it is a Malinnov."

"Meaning?"

"Malaysian innovation! Malinnov Pistols are made in Kuala Lumpur."

"What?"

"Do you have any enemy or know any person from Malaysia?"

The officer asked Neel and the first person that struck him was Jeeva Velu Stane. Then he dismissed the thought. He had liked Jeeva and he could not have been so wrong about judging people.

"No, I don't know anyone."

"Then we will start the search. Meanwhile if you find anyone suspicious, do inform us."

****

Sindhoora was winding up her work for the day when Mouna, the receptionist approached her.

"Hi guess what?"

"What?" Sindhoora asked the girl who appeared chirpy and blithe always.

"The handsome dude, who took you for coffee, was crestfallen when I told him that you are not single."

"What?"

Mouna giggled and continued animatedly, "Yes, I wish he had asked me out. I know you have a boyfriend and he looked dejected when you gave him your piece of mind."

"But Mouna, I do not have a boyfriend. Why did you tell him that?"

"What? But you do, right? That guy who comes to office to pick you up…Isn't he your boyfriend?"

"No Mouna, he is my cousin. He is not my boyfriend. And I am single," Sindhoora reiterated, annoyed with Mouna's assumption about Akhil.

"Oh, but Sindhu, your cousin told me once that you both were planning to get married to each other. Hence I assumed that you were going steady."

"When did he say that?"

"I don't remember exactly but quite recently. I think he had come to pick you up, but you got late. He told me casually."

Sindhoora fumed at Akhil's audacity. How dare he go about declaring that they were planning to marry? She wanted to have a word with him.

"So why did you turn down Jeeva's invitation?"

"He was conceited and over-confident! I am uncomfortable with such guys," Sindhoora replied.

"Guys? Sindhu darling, he was not just a guy. He was one of the best specimens of a virile male."

Sindhoora could not help but grin at her friend's description of Jeeva Velu Stane, "So why didn't you ask him out?"

"Well, he was simply not interested in me. I tried to flirt with him, but he had eyes only for you." Mouna sighed with regret.

Sindhoora laughed at her friend's loud sigh. Everyone in the office found Mouna interesting and most of the men liked to chat with her because she made them laugh with her funny and mock accents and anecdotes. She always had a funny story to narrate and it involved invariably one of the top brass.

Reaching home, Sindhoora tried calling Akhil but his phone was switched off. So, she decided to talk to him the next day.

****

Neel was deep in thought when he reached his house. The officer had asked him to consider every acquaintance or friend who could have acquired the pistol from Malaysia. He decided to consult Nedumaran.

The outhouse was dark, and he knocked the door, but no one opened it. So, he threw open the door and switched on the lights.

The room was empty. Neel searched the whole house, but he could not find Nedumaran. He called the security to enquire if Nedumaran left the premise, but they denied seeing Nedumaran. He heard the sound of dripping water and rushed to the bathroom. The tap was half-open but there was no sign of Nedumaran. When he turned around, he halted in shock. The words scrawled in bold letters on the back of the door with a wet soap stunned him.

"Your enemy is inside your house…"

24) WHO WAS THE ENEMY?

"With doe-eyes and resplendent face, she revels in his cosmic dance while the demigods and sages from all the worlds bow their heads in praise." Thirumurai 6 (1-3)

Sindhoora's phone buzzed,

"Hi, Jeeva here"

"How did you get the number?"

"Look how I got the number is not important. What is more relevant is the way I behaved at the office. I am sorry Sindhoora. I know I behaved like an ass. I should not have."

Sindhoora was quiet but his apologetic tone reminded her of Mouna's description of him. She smiled as she recollected her words.

"It is not that important." Sindhoora stressed 'not that important' deliberately.

"I get it," Jeeva replied and there was an awkward silence. Sindhoora debated whether to end the call or say something.

"Look, forget that meeting. Let us make peace. I genuinely want us to be friends. Is that alright?'

"I think so."

"Great. I am working this Friday night at *Rhythms*. And it is a special night because of the long weekend. There is a party at the venue, and I will be playing some special numbers. Why don't you come?"

Jeeva's invitation surprised Sindhoora but she had never visited a pub or DJ party and even if she had wanted to, her father would not allow her to go late night to such parties.

"Thanks, but I can't come."

"Why not? I can send you the invite."

"Sorry Jeeva. Some other time perhaps…" With that, Sindhoora concluded the call. Actually, she would not mind visiting a pub. She had heard interesting stories about such places from some of her friends, but she was a little hesitant to ask her father's permission. Hence she decided to forego the invitation.

****

Neel stared at the words scrawled on the back of the door with a wet soap. He searched the two rooms for some clues. Had Nedumaran walked away from the house of his own volition or was he kidnapped? If he had written the words on the back of the door, was it not possible that someone had abducted him. Neel found the old man's bag under the bed while searching for personal belongings. The pouch of gold coins was untouched. There was also a diary and a change of clothes. Neel carried the items to his room. He flicked through the pages of the diary. There were verses of old hymns and songs scribbled on some of the pages. He placed Nedumaran's belongings in his closet and realized that Nedumaran was taken against his will. If the old man had gone on his own, he would not have left his personal possessions behind. Who was this enemy inside the house? He paced the room restlessly and he ventured into the balcony. His sweeping glance observed the security at the gate, the hounds moving about the garden, but his attention was drawn to the man who was leaving the house through the main entrance. His long strides took him quickly to the man. The man was startled by the barrage of questions that Neel threw at him, leading to Neel's realization that the man was a pharmacist who had come to deliver his grandfather's medicines. Neel let the man out. He approached the security at the gate and asked them to play the CCTV recording. Neel observed that there was nothing out of the ordinary in the recording. So how did Nedumaran leave? He prowled around the garden with the hounds at his heels. While checking the outhouse gates, his attention was caught by the small wicket gate at one end of the garden, about which he had forgotten. There were no CCTV cameras fitted here. The exit led to the bylane of the main road and it was usually quiet and deserted. Was Nedumaran kidnapped through this exit?

Back inside his house, he decided to observe all the servants unobtrusively. Nedumaran hinted about an enemy in the house. And all at once, the house seemed oppressive with too many secrets and memories of his cousin. Neel hurried out of the house and went for a long drive to clear his head.

****

Nedumaran woke up to pitch darkness. His hands and legs were tied and eyes blindfolded. He let his mind focus on the sounds and realised that it was the wee hours before dawn. Where was he? Not in the city because there was unusual quietness that would not have prevailed in any city, even if it was the crack of dawn. And who did this to him? He could not think of anyone who would bundle him away like this. Unless they were the ones with whom he fought on that day, a week ago, in the estate. A team of four or five people had descended on the estate to measure the ground and discuss plans to build ostentatious structures on it. When he found them, he had become so furious that he had lashed at them verbally. After they left the premises, he had taken the first train to Chennai and reached Arunachalam's house. Would Neel see the words he had written on the door? He was sure that somebody from the house had added poison to his food. This made him ponder if the property in Chidambaram was put on the market by the family of Arunachalam. The thin ray of light through the tiny gap in the door revealed that morning had broken. Nedumaran was curious to find his abductor. He did not care about his well-being, but he was worried for the safety of Revathi's son Nilagriva. He was certain that the person who kidnapped him was a confederate of an organized crime.

****

Neel was nowhere near finding Nedumaran. The old man was still absconding or rather abducted. Neel had no clue. He checked the outhouse a number of times, but he had come up with nothing. Moreover, he had to take his mother for dressing to the clinic. His father had left for an official trip and Mahesh was attending a seminar today.

While driving back from the hospital, his mother asked him about Nedumaran, "Neel where is that old friend of your grandfather who arrived from Chidambaram yesterday?"

Neel hesitated before answering his mother, "He is staying at the outhouse."

"Oh, he seemed an interesting man," his mother spoke her thought aloud and he looked at her with curiosity.

"Really?"

"Yes, the first question he asked when we met was about my injury."

Neel was amused that Nedumaran had made an impression on his mother.

"Maybe he was trying to impress you. You are a beautiful woman," Neel suggested with a grin and his mother flushed at the compliment, "Neel, what are you saying?"

Neel laughed at her embarrassment, but he was concerned about the absent Nedumaran. He had been missing for more than twelve hours. After dropping his mother home, he drove to the corporate office of *Thillai Group of Industries.* He had set up a cabin for himself in one of the executive floors but this morning his mind was not on his work. He opened his laptop and searched for information on the city of Chidambaram and its suburbs. After an hour of search, he could find nothing useful. There were the usual updates from innumerable tourist websites about temple visits and boat rides in the wetlands. His cell phone rang. It was Ann.

It was the last day of her India visit, and Ann was unhappy to say goodbye to Neel.

"Neel, when are you coming back to the U.S? You know Arnie is leaving for a vacation in a couple of weeks," Ann reminded Neel of one of their partners' holiday plans. Neel sighed…

"Yes, I know. He called me yesterday. Ann, I won't be able to come for next three months at least. You and Michael have to manage without me and Arnie for some days."

"Is there a family emergency Neel?"

"Kind of…" Neel did not give any details.

"Your company in the U.S too needs you Neel. You can't ignore it after setting it up with so much effort and pains. Our clients seek your advice and you are the face of the organization."

His intercom buzzed… "Just hold on Ann…"

"Yes"

"There is a visitor for you Neel…." The middle-aged woman who attended the front desk informed him. On his first visit to the office, he had asked everyone to call him Neel instead of '*Sir*'.

"Who is it?"

"Sindhoora Vaidyanathan"

Neel caught his breath at the name. "Let her come" he instructed.

"Hello" Ann's voice reminded him that he was holding her call.

"Ann, I need to go. Have a safe journey. I will catch up with you soon," Neel tried to end the call, but Ann continued to point out the need for his presence at the American office.

Neel was not listening to her because his eyes were fixed on the entrance of the lounge through the cabin glass.

"Neel, are you listening?" Ann spoke loudly and he ended the call as Sindhoora stepped out of the elevator tentatively. In a long white embroidered *kurta* and blue tights, she had draped her blue stole around her neck casually. She looked chic with her hair drawn back into a single plait that rested over her shoulder. Clasping a folder tightly she stood in hesitation gripping the strap of the bag. Someone pointed out his cabin and she approached uncertainly.

Neel pulled his loosened tie in place when she knocked on his door.

She stepped inside as he watched her, and her gentle smile warmed his heart.

"Hi…"

"Come in."

"Sorry to barge in like this but I needed to discuss something very important with you," she said after taking the seat.

"Did your bosses send you?"

"My boss does not know that I am here. I have excused myself for a couple of hours from office."

His phone vibrated and it was Ann again. He disconnected the call while Sindhoora glanced around his office. It was simple and efficient. A coffee machine and desktop were the only items in the room.

"Will you have coffee?"

"No thanks. Actually, I wanted to ask you about this property you own in Chidambaram," she came straight to the point.

Neel leaned back on the chair waiting for her to continue. Her lashes were dark and long, and her nose was as cute as button. But it was her wide eyes that drew his attention. Her gaze was sharp, yet they betrayed none of her feelings. She opened her folder and extracted a document. Her fingers were long, and a thin bracelet rested on her slender wrist. The chunky earrings made of silver dangled against her chin.

"See this is the property I was talking about," she handed him the document and he looked through them. Sindhoora explained, "I understand that you are planning to sell the property but…"

Neel's phone vibrated once more and Sindhoora glanced at it. The name Ann was displayed but Neel ignored the call, concentrating on the document.

"Aren't you going to answer your phone?" Sindhoora asked when the caller seemed determined to talk to Neel.

Neel grabbed the phone and switched it off. He looked at her and said, "This is our ancestral property in the outskirts of the town. I was not aware that this estate was up for sale."

"But didn't you discuss it with our chairman on your last visit?"

"I am not sure if we discussed about this particular property. I learnt the details of this property only recently."

"If I tell you something, I hope you will not mind…" Sindhoora appealed and at his encouraging nod she continued.

"Your estate lies on a very valued stretch of land. Developing it into a resort or for any other commercial purpose would lead to the destruction of the mangroves that run along the property."

Neel stared at her as he felt a sense of Déjà vu. Nedumaran had made a similar appeal to him last night.

"What do you know about this property?" Neel asked Sindhoora.

"Not much but my grandmother once told me that the area around the mangroves is a blessed piece of land." Sindhoora did not enlighten him about the deeply held secret of her grandmother. Right now, she had only one aim and that was to protect that piece of land and the mangroves from land grabbers.

Neel regarded Sindhoora thoughtfully wondering if she had heard about the mythical pool or keys. "Have you heard anything else about this land?" Neel asked her curiously

"Should I have?"

"Since you are the one who is appealing to me to safeguard this property, I am wondering if you know something more about it."

Sindhoora was in two minds. Should she tell him about the ancient tale of the Pool, leaving out her grandmother's connection or should she refrain from mentioning it to anyone, even if it happened to be the owner of the property?

The myriad of expressions flitting across her face captivated Neel and he could not look away from her. There was something so intoxicating about gazing into her eyes that he felt he was gliding outside the realm of his physical existence. Finally, she looked at him and he held his breath at the vividness of her eyes that gleamed like a stormy sky. He felt an irresistible urge to wipe away that twinge of trouble and bring the sparkle back to her eyes. He reflected about the man on the bike he had seen with her the other day. What was her relationship with him?

"No, I just want to make sure that the mangroves are protected. I am appealing to you to keep the land and not let it out for redevelopment."

Neel frowned and said thoughtfully, "I do not think that the property has been let out for development. Let me check it out."

"Thank you. And one more thing, please do not mention my visit to anyone in my office. I know it is not ethical of me to speak directly to the client, but I was concerned about the property." She was aware that she was chattering meaninglessly, but Neel disturbed her composure. He didn't speak much but his dark and brooding eyes made her nervous. She didn't know how she gathered the courage to come to his office, but some instinct had encouraged her to appeal to him. After all he was the one who owned the property.

"Relax, I won't. But I should thank you for warning me about the impending problem. I will certainly check the details of the property."

Sindhoora stood up abruptly, "I should be leaving." She collected her folder and bag. Neel stood up too. "Maybe we should discuss this in detail over coffee," Neel suggested casually and Sindhoora paused. They stared at each other across the table and Neel came around the table, offering his hand. Sindhoora's delicate palm was engulfed in his larger hand. She could smell his aftershave that was a mixture of musk and lemon. His strong jaw was smooth and clean-shaved. When her eyes caught his, she shivered at the appreciation glinting in his eyes. Or was it more than appreciation? She was not sure, but he excited her. She held her breath as he stepped aside for her to move on. She hoped that she would not make a fool of herself. He reached the door before she did and held it open for her. When she passed through the door, he said, "Take care Sindhoora. I will call you after learning the details of the property."

She nodded quietly and strode away from his cabin. Only when she reached the elevator did she let out a long breath. Her pulses raced at the way he uttered her name. Not many people called her full name. Most of them abbreviated it to Sindhu. But the way Neel said her name, she felt as if he enjoyed saying it.

25) SRI KALAHASTI

"Infinite as he is without birth or death, those mindless of metempsychosis and roaming in filth will not endear themselves to him." Thirumurai 6 (3-5)

Almost the entire population of the town of *Sri Kalahasti* had assembled at the temple for the *Rahu-Ketu pooja*. The fact that the Pooja was conducted by one of the established and prominent families of the town was enough to encourage most of the families to be in attendance at the ancient temple built in 5th century by the *Pallavi* dynasty, although the construction period lasted centuries with contributions from other ruling dynasties such as the *Chola and Vijayanagar* empires. One of the *Pancha Bootha Sthalam* (five elements), *Kalahasti* temple has the Lord Shiva as the presiding deity in the form of *Vaayu (air) lingam*. The temple was also associated with *Rahu and Ketu* pooja, believed to dispel the ill effects of these malevolent heavenly bodies on people's lives.

DSP Ranjan Rao was concerned about the growing number of people in the temple premises. His team was already present to supervise the event, but one could never be lax about the mood of the crowd. The family, which was performing the religious event, was politically connected and had a powerful background. So, he had come from *Chittoor* to overlook the affair personally. One of the businesses that the family held was a textile printing unit that specialized in a traditional form called *Kalamkari*. The traditional print that was made out of fast vegetable dye had been recently revived by a group of artists across the country, and the temple town, famous for the artwork, was once again in demand for its *Kalamkari* work on clothes with stories from epics like *Ramayana* and *Mahabharata*. Some of them specialized in other stories and folklores. Ranjan learnt that most of the families thronging the venue were *Kalamkari* artists.

It was when the head priest concluded the ceremony that Ranjan's mobile phone began ringing.

He exited from the pillared hall to answer the call that was from the head of the town's police station.

"Hello?"

"Sir, I got a call from one of the residents about a family that has been locked in a house since last night…"

"Which area?"

"Near *Sannidhi street*…"

Ranjan Rao frowned at the location. It was a crowded and old street near the main temple tower.

"Inform me about the developments."

An hour later when most of the guests had moved to the main courtyard for meals, Ranjan received another call from the same officer.

"Sir, you have to come here as soon as possible."

"Why? What is the matter Pradip?"

"Sir I can't tell you. I will message you the address. It is urgent."

When Ranjan reached the house, there was already a crowd of people in front of the gate. Ranjan had guessed earlier that there was something seriously wrong after Pradip spoke to him. But he did not reckon the ghastly sight that awaited him. The house was cordoned off by the police and an ambulance had arrived. Pradip guided him towards the first floor through a flight of narrow steps.

Ranjan's legs ceased to move in shock at the horrifying sight. He saw four bodies hanging from the ceiling with their hands tied at the back and eyes blindfolded. Two women, a man and a boy were suspended from the beam that ran along the ceiling by a noose in their necks.

"Sir, there is one more." Pradip took him to another small room where an old woman lay dead with her throat slit open.

"My god Pradip! Who did this?"

"It seems like multiple suicides. They were in deep debt."

"But this woman was murdered," Ranjan pointed at the old woman.

"I think they murdered her first and then committed suicide. And there are no thefts."

"How do you know?"

"Sir, there is no forced entry, and everything seems to be in order."

"Hmm…" Ranjan did not believe that they had committed suicide, but he did not voice his theory. He let the officers do their duty, while he prowled around the house, looking for clues. Even if they had committed suicide, how did the last member blindfold himself, tie his hands and hang himself from the beam? Moreover, he had observed the fresh scar on the back of the man's neck. He was certain that the investigating officers too would notice it and make their own conclusions. And why was the old woman killed? Was it because she protested against their decision to end lives? In the second room, there were rolls of running material. And there were frames with designs and prints. He realised that they were *kalamkari* artists. He opened the cupboard and found brushes, dyes and rolls of prints. He moved to another room where there were more cans of paints, rolls of materials and brushes. Pradip met him after his enquiries with neighbors.

"Sir, they were *kalamkari* artists and they specialized in *Nayanar* folklores…"

"What folklores?"

"Sir, *Nayanars! Nayanars* were saints who spread *Shaivism* during the 4th, 5th and 6th centuries. And they hailed from Tamil Nadu. This family's mother tongue was Tamil."

"So, they worked only on *Nayanar* tales and not anything else?"

"No, nothing else! Usually the *Kalamkari* work depicted tales from either *Ramayana or Mahabharata* but this was the only family who printed stories from *Shiva Puranam*. And they were in deep debt. They did not work for any particular unit. They did freelance work and the family travelled with their work to distant towns to sell their pieces. Unlike other artists here, they did not conform themselves to any set up."

"And the suicide theory? Is it true?"

"Prima facie, it looks like suicide sir. The neighbours are saying that the family had been worried about the dwindling finances and lack of demand for their work."

Letting Pradip answer the questions from the press, Ranjan searched the house for photos and clues. He could find nothing but when he was about to leave the room, a worn-out diary thrown in the bin caught his eye. He retrieved it and carried it with him to the station. He was leaving for *Chittoor* that night so he would hand it over to the investigating officer, but he wanted to read it before anyone did. He leafed through the diary while travelling back to the guest house and found some hymns and verses. He clicked their pictures and saved it in his phone. They were not written in a language he could read. He was not familiar with Tamil, although he understood it a little if someone spoke to him.

****

When the blindfold was removed, it took his eyes some time to adjust to the jarring brightness of mid afternoon. A plate of food was thrust at him and Nedumaran was allowed to use the washroom. But he had no idea where he was confined, and no one approached him to discuss the significance of his situation. When he could focus his eyes, he looked at the muscled man who was talking softly on the phone. He assumed that he was the one who had abducted him from Nilagriva's house. The man's back was broad and strong and when he turned around, Nedumaran caught his breath at the familiar scarred face. It was Ponmalan. He sold drugs in Chidambaram and other towns. Nedumaran had caught him red-handed once while he was trying to sell his drugs to a minor. Nedumaran had apprehended him for his transgression. Now he looked at the younger man and asked,

"Why have you kidnapped me? And you are the one who killed Shreekant, aren't you?

Ponmalan stared at him angrily and left the room, banging the door behind him.

****

Next morning, the press covered the story of the multiple suicides on their front page and Chandra Shekhar who was on an official trip

248

to Hyderabad from Chennai was appalled at the news item. He called up his old friend Ranjan Rao to enquire about the matter and he was distressed to know that the family was a Tamil speaking one.

"Chandra Shekhar, where are you now?"

"I am in Hyderabad, but I am travelling back to Chennai tomorrow. Why?"

"I need your help to translate something written in Tamil. I will be coming to Chennai this Friday. Can we meet?"

"Of course! Give me a call and we will head to our old place." Chandra Shekhar mentioned the old restaurant near the college they had attended years ago.

"Does it still exist?" Ranjan asked in surprise.

"You will be surprised to see the revamped one."

They decided to meet on Friday at their old haunt.

****

It was Friday afternoon and Sindhoora remembered that it was the night that Jeeva had invited her for his gig. She sighed. She had refused his invitation flagrantly, but she wished she had accepted it. Since meeting Neel at his office, she was restless and edgy. She had been waiting for him to call her to discuss the estate at Chidambaram but so far he had not spoken to her. Now as she mulled over Jeeva's invitation, Akhil called her.

"Hi Sindhu"

"Hi"

"You said you wanted to discuss something with me."

"Yeah, can we meet this evening?" Sindhoora had wanted to spare him from the predicament of outright rejection but he seemed to harbour hopes of convincing her to love him. Her talk with the receptionist laid bare the fact that he assumed her to be his fiancée and was declaring it to everyone.

"Sure, I will come to pick you up at the office, maybe around seven."

****

By seven that evening, Sindhoora waited for Akhil in the lobby. Most of her co-workers had left and she plugged her earphones with her favourite playlist as she lingered. The song was one of her favourites and she loved the soulful rendition of the original playback singer. With her eyes closed, she enjoyed the song composed in a mixture of Carnatic ragas like *Arabhi* and *Bilahari*. She loved the way the song veered towards raga *Yadukula Kamboji* at places. She hummed along with the original in her modulated low voice.

Yearning for shield,

You came to me with protection,

Like a song from the soul

You soothed my bruise

Like a balm, your eyes

Assuaged the pain and

Your love was the blessing

I craved for….

Absorbed in the melody, she did not see the man entering the lobby just then, who paused at the sight of Sindhoora. Enraptured by her singing, his gaze was fixed on her face.

When the song ended she opened her eyes and froze in embarrassment. They stared at each other, a significant moment as they recognized the attraction they held for each other.

"Hi…" Neel greeted.

"Hi……" She wanted to ask what he was doing here but she seemed tongue-tied at the moment as if she was unwilling to break the spell.

"I tried calling you today, but your phone was either switched off or unanswered," he explained, taking in her appearance in jeans and long shirt. His quick glance encompassed her outfit, hairstyle and face. He noticed that she had used dark kohl to highlight her eyes. There was something about her eyes that entranced him always.

"Did you?" She checked her phone for missed calls. But before she could give him a reply, he advanced slowly towards her and asked, "If you are done for the day, can we go somewhere for coffee? We can discuss that matter about the estate." The estate was the last thing on his mind then.

"Actually, I am waiting for someone," she replied and as if on cue, Akhil entered the lobby with his helmet in his hand. He stopped when he saw Neel and Sindhoora together at the lobby.

"Sorry Sindhu, I got a little late. Shall we go?" He asked dismissing Neel with a glance.

"Hi, I am Neel Chandra." Sindhoora was surprised by Neel's voluntary introduction and Akhil was compelled to reciprocate the greeting.

"Akhil…" They shook hands as Sindhoora watched them. Akhil gave a tight smile at Neel and turned to her, "Shall we go Sindhu?"

The way he called her '*Sindhu*', grated on Neel's nerves. He disliked the pompous ass. And something about the way he looked at Sindhoora provoked Neel to issue the invitation.

"I invited Sindhoora for coffee. Care to join us?" He asked Akhil and took sadistic pleasure at the way Akhil's face flushed with anger at his brazen offer. Akhil turned to look at Sindhoora and she flicked an angry glance at Neel. She wondered what game Neel was playing.

"Perhaps some other time…" she replied and prompted Akhil to leave. Akhil was only too happy to escape from the brooding guy called Neel who was not taking his eyes off Sindhoora. With a resentful glance at Neel, he took hold of Sindhoora's hand and walked out of the lobby. Sindhoora did not want to create a scene in front of Neel so she tailed after Akhil and snatched her hand away once they were out of Neel's earshot.

Akhil kicked the bike to ignition and asked, "Where shall we go?"

Sindhoora said the first name that came to her mind, "*Rhythm and Sounds*"

Neel glared after them, enraged over the way Sindhoora was yanked by her friend. Who the hell did he think he was? He had tried to be friendly even though he detested the man's possessive hold on Sindhoora. And why did she not resist him? Neel did not think that she could be taken for granted by any person. No, he guessed that she did not want to make a scene in front of him. Anyway, he was coming back to the office the next day so he would talk to her then. Right now, he needed a mug of chilled beer to cool his temper. That reminded him that his friend Jeeva had invited him for the party tonight at the pub.

****

Chandra Shekhar and Ranjan Rao met at their old haunt and relived their college memories. Over dinner and drinks, they discussed their work, family and lives.

"So Ranjan; what help can I do for you?"

"Remember the multiple suicides in *Kalahasti* a couple of days ago?"

"Yes Yes, I remember. Did you make any progress in the case? Why did they commit suicide?"

"I don't think it was suicide Chandra. My gut instinct tells me that it was homicide, but we have not got any evidence to suggest otherwise."

"Oh yes, the suicide theory seems dubious."

"I know. I got hold of a diary, but it had nothing useful except for some old verses and hymns. They were written in Tamil and I needed your help to translate them."

"Sure, why not? Show me," Chandra Shekhar suggested and Ranjan extracted his mobile phone to show the pictures he had clicked. He enlarged the pictures and showed them to his friend.

"See this Chandra, what do these lines mean? This was the last entry made in the diary."

Chandra Shekhar read the lines aloud,

"The King of the tongue was saved by the holy bull,

Even if he did a lot of misdeeds due to ignorance,

But your boy could not be saved by the evil pull,

That destroyed him due to their emergence...."

And then he stopped in sickening shock as the significance of the words hit him with shattering horror.

He looked up at Ranjan and whispered in appalled fear, "Dear god Ranjan! I have seen this verse in a message sent to me before..."

To be continued .....

BOOK II

A Blue Moon Interlude

THE VERSE

After their visit to the main shrine, Jeeva and Neel strolled around the temple admiring the architecture and view of the hills.

"Neel, let us walk around the hills. The guide was suggesting that it is the most scenic part of the town."

Neel was impatient to continue with the journey but he complied with Jeeva's request.

They exited the fourth *Prakaram* and faced another enormous *Nandi* in another *mandapam*. They paused to look closely at the stone sculpture. Unexpectedly, an old man with a long white beard and a dash of vermillion on his forehead approached them. He tapped Neel's hand and gave a kind smile. The aged man reminded Neel of the missing Nedumaran.

"Are you new to this town?" He asked Neel and when Neel nodded, he suggested "Why don't you boys go to that 1000 pillared hall? It is a beautiful hall with many engravings on the pillars."

Neel and Jeeva were amused when the old man addressed them as boys. Neel looked at the *Mandapam* that the man pointed out. Jeeva got curious and asked, "You mean there are 1000 pillars?"

"Yes, in olden times every temple had such a *mandapam* so that the residents could take refuge in such halls during war, raids or natural calamity."

"Oh interesting. Neel, can we see it?" They proceeded towards the hall.

The door to the hall was open and Jeeva rushed inside to view the pillared hall. Before Neel stepped in, he turned back to look at the old man who had suggested the hall but he was nowhere to be seen. Neel searched the crowded courtyard but he could not spot him. The bearded man had disappeared.

"Are there really 1000 pillars?" Jeeva asked Neel and wandered around the hall, admiring the carvings on the pillars.

The pillars, erected centuries ago, stood in silent glory emanating power and valour. Even dank smell of stone could not contain the charming aura of mystery that pervaded the hall. The brilliance of the engineering astounded Neel and Jeeva.

"Neel, look at the beast carved on this pillar. The body of a lion but the face of an elephant! What an imagination! Brilliant!"

"It must have been the symbol of a ruling dynasty," Neel commented-

"Yes, it must have been. After all there were many empires that ruled the town."

Many of the pillars had many inscriptions in Tamil. Neel viewed them closely and clicked pictures of them. He translated them using an app on his phone. The verses praised the presiding Lord of the temple and town.

"Lord Shiva who is the trove of wisdom and knowledge,
Resides in the hills of Annamalai,
Where flocks of bear and deer
Gather at night for shelter....Thirumurai 1(69-3)

Neel ran his eyes on the engravings of the pillars while Jeeva admired the carvings. Neel stopped at one pillar where the words seemed familiar as if he had seen them before.

He froze in shock as he went closer and read the verse once again with an uncanny feeling of danger lurking around him.

"The King of the tongue was saved by the holy bull,
Even if he did a lot of misdeeds due to ignorance,
But your boy could not be saved by the evil pull,
That destroyed him due to their emergence…."

****

GLOSSARY

Word	Meaning
Aanaimalai hills or Anamala hills	Also known as the Elephant Mountains, they are the range of mountains that form the southern portion of the Western Ghats and span the border of Tamil Nadu and Kerala in Southern India.
Acharya	Spiritual teacher
Adyar	A suburb in South Chennai
Agraharams	A street that was traditionally the Brahmin quarter of a heterogeneous village in South India, or the name of any village inhabited by Brahmins. The houses were built on land donated by noble men or kings, to families particularly Brahmins who performed religious duties in temples.
Alangaram	Adorning of the goddess
Anna	Elder Brother
Anni	Sister-in-law
Appavan Kandan	One of the sons of the sentinel guarding the Healing Pool who travelled to the temple town of Thiruvanaikaval with the famed key
Arudhra Darisanam	*See Thiruvadirai*
Bharathiyar	Popular Tamil poet and Indian independence activist cum social reformer
Chamiers Road	An upmarket area in Chennai
Chithi	Aunt
Deepa aradhanai	A ceremonial waving of lamps illuminating the deity, with camphor or with a deepam - oil or clarified butter lamps
Dupatta	Indian clothing accessory similar to stole
Ellu Urandai & Nei Appams	A dish of sesame seeds balls and a sweet dish made of jaggery and flour
Homam	a ritual where religious offering is made into fire on special occasions, festivals or functions
Kamal Haasan	Famous Tamil movie star
Kanaka Sabhai	Among the many Shiva temples, five temples - Chidambaram, Madurai, Thiruvilankadu,

Word	Meaning
	Tirunelveli and Kutralam - are very revered and known as the five 'sabhas'. It is said Lord Shiva has danced at these five places as Nataraja - the dancing form of Shiva, to benefit different devotees. The temple at Chidambaram is known as Ponnambalam - Gold Sabha or the Kanaka Sabha.
Kancheevaram	A small temple town near Chennai famous for its silk weaving industry and the silk sarees that it produces
Khadi	A hand-woven natural fibre cloth
Khajuraho	Famous monuments in Madhya Pradesh, India, a UNESCO World Heritage site, built between 950 AD and 1050 AD by the Chandela dynasty, which are famous for their erotic sculptures
Kodi Marams	Flag poles placed between the Rajagopuram (Gateway of the temple) and the Sanctum Sanctorum in Hindu temples in the southern part of India
Lingam	An iconic representation of Lord Shiva
Lord Nataraja and Goddess Sivakami	Lord Siva in his dancing form and his consort
Maha Abhishekam	Grand ritual of bathing the Lord
Mahabalipuram	Also known as Mamallapuram, is a coastal town near Chennai known for the UNESCO World Heritage Site of 7th and 8th century Hindu Monuments
Mahadeva	Another name for lord Shiva
Maharajapuram Santhanam	A popular South Indian classical singer
Mandapam	Roofed hall, typically found in ancient temples
Margazhi	The month in the Tamil Calendar that falls in December-January
Mylapore	Old residential neighbourhood in the central part of Chennai
Nayanars	A group of 63 saints (saint poets) in Tamil Nadu during 6th to 8th century who were

Word	Meaning
	devoted to Lord Shiva
Om namah shivaya	A customary chant invoking the blessings of Lord Shiva. 'Om' is believed to be a sacred sound in Hinduism
Oonjal	A swing that is anchored to the ceiling of a room. Iron chains connect the wooden plank to the hooks in the ceiling, often used as furniture in south Indian homes
Paati	Grandmother
Paavadai	A traditional long skirt worn by girls in South India
Pancha Bhootha Sthal	Pancha means five, Bootha means elements, Sthalam means place; refer to five temples dedicated to Lord Shiva, each representing an element of nature. The five primary elements of nature are - Sky, water, earth, fire and air. Four temples are located in Tamil Nadu and the fifth one is in Andhra Pradesh
Panguni	The last month of the Tamil Calendar
Pichavaram Mangroves	Pichavaram is a village near Chidamabaram which houses the second largest mangrove forest covering 1100 hectares of area
Prasadams	Food traditionally offered to God during prayers
Rahasiya Puja	Ritual of secret worship, unique to the Chidambaram temple
Ragam-Tanam-Pallavi	Form of improvisational rendering in Carnatic music
Royapettah	Commercial district in Chennai
Siddhars	Saints in India, who were mostly Shiva worshippers and practised spiritual penance to attain liberation.
Thai Pongal	Festival of harvest celebrated in Tamil Nadu in the month of January
Thatha	Grandfather
Thillai Forest	Thillai trees are an extinct variety of *Exoceria Agollacha* which used to grow in the wetlands of Pichavaram.
Thiruvadirai Festival or Thiruvathirai	A Hindu festival celebrated in Tamil Nadu and Kerala. It takes place on the full moon night in the Tamil month of Margazhi

Word	Meaning
or Arudhra Darisanam	(December–January) and this is also the longest night in a year. Literary and historical evidence in the form of stone inscriptions state that the festival has been celebrated on this day for more than 1500 years. Thiruvathirai (Arudhra) means "sacred big wave", using which this universe was created by Lord Shiva about 132 trillion years ago. In Thillai Chidambaram, the Festival is held for 10 days and on the 9th night (i.e., 10th day very early morning) the Maha Abhishekam is done to Lord Nataraja and Goddess Sivakamisundari at Raja Sabhai (royal hall) at around 3 am. The MahaAbhishekam (the bathing ritual of the God) is held for about 3–4 hours. Then special Thiruvabaranam (Sacred Jewels) Alankaram (decoration), Rahasiya Pujai (secret worship) is done to Sri Natarajar
Vakil	A lawyer
Vanakkam	A respectful greeting
Vangiyam	An ancient wind instrument played during auspicious occasions in South India
Veshti	A traditional men's garment in the form of a rectangular and long piece of unstitched cloth, wrapped around the waist, typically worn in South India
Vilvam	Commonly known as 'Belpatra' in Hindi, it is a kind of leaf offered in worship to Lord Shiva

ABOUT THE AUTHOR

Viji is an educationist by profession. One of the reasons for her successful stint as a teacher was her story-telling sessions which her students looked forward to. Their keen interest in her stories led to her writing, a passion that she discovered a few years back. Viji loves to tell stories about the essence of human nature and the role it plays in larger social issues. She takes keen interest in discussions on international disputes, climate change issues and conflicts of human rights.

Her first work, based on a popular television show, garnered 113k views, 6k likes and almost 300 comments on digital platforms. Her other publishing credits include, "Tempest Love" & "Wild Summer Echoes" which garnered overwhelming reader response.

Viji believes that there is a story in every house, every village and every town. Her dream is to write novels that represent the vibrant heritage of every state in India. Capturing the varied cultures and weaving their richness together to create stories is her aspiration.

Email   : Viji67mum@gmail.com

Website : Viji67mum.blogspot.com

Twitter : @Viji_Musings

Facebook : Viji Venkat

Instagram : vijivenkat89